# BAD MAN'S TOWN

## Al Cody

CHIVERS LARGE PRINT
BATH

**Library of Congress Cataloging-in-Publication Data**

Cody, Al, 1899–
  Bad man's town / Al Cody.
    p.   cm.
  ISBN  0–7927–1492–X
  ISBN  0–7927–1491–1 (pbk.)
  1. Large type books.  I. Title.
[PS3519.O712B3  1993]           92–37981
813′.54—dc20                        CIP

**British Library Cataloguing in Publication Data available**

This Large Print edition is published by Chivers Press, England, and by Curley Large Print, an imprint of Chivers North America, 1993.

Published by arrangement with Donald MacCampbell, Inc.

U.K. Hardcover  ISBN  0 7451 1811 9
U.K. Softcover  ISBN  0 7451 1822 4
U.S. Hardcover  ISBN  0 7927 1492 X
U.S. Softcover  ISBN  0 7927 1491 1

*Printed in Great Britain*

# CONTENTS

# BAD MAN'S TOWN

# CHAPTER ONE

# A STRANGE DEAL

The moon, high above rearing canyon walls, was spending its last quarter with a miserly hand. Scant light penetrated these depths, and the cabin, crouching under shrouding pines and the overhang of the cliff, had been planned as a hide-out. Jim Thornton, 'Gentleman Jim,' moving like one of the shadows, slipped on the flat stone before the door. Something greasy and slimy to the touch was underfoot. Looking carefully, he recognized it for a patch of half-dried blood.

*And the blood is the life*, he thought swiftly. *Whose, I wonder?* Only once before had he been to this hideout cabin, and that a long time ago, but he knew who was supposed to be there now, and his mind darted ahead to the three known occupants. To Happy, long his own partner in games of chance, who was here, if report had it correctly, as a prisoner and a hostage for his own appearance.

*If they've hurt Happy*—he thought grimly, and left the notion unfinished for the moment. The blood might belong to the Weasel, of course, as sinewy and sinister and twice as bloodthirsty as the animal for

1

which he had been nicknamed. If it was his blood spilled here, no one would care.

Nor would anyone be likely to grieve if it was that of Big Nose, who liked to call himself The Boss. Though Big Nose had his moments. Gentleman Jim gave no thought to the fact that he was virtually inviting the spilling of his own blood by coming here as demanded.

Still, the pool might belong to someone else. He listened, but the night had no tongues. There was no light under the door, but that too was customary, for he remembered a hallway inside, and that would be left dark for safety's sake.

He entered now, pausing in that black entryway as voices came from the room beyond. A yellow thread of light marked the second door, and the voices were familiar. The door was thrown abruptly open and light flooded out and the Weasel stood framed there, a six-gun clutched in one hand.

For a moment he glared, lips drawn back from nervous teeth. Then his breath expelled in a sibilant hiss.

'Ah-h! It's you, Thornton! Come on in.'

'Who did you expect?' Gentleman Jim asked mildly. He stood for a moment in turn, framed in the doorway, filling it, an easy and graceful six feet. He had the eye of an eagle, now mildly curious as it ranged the room, with the nose below it somewhat reminiscent of the same bird. His hair, sideburns and moustache were all one with the outer night.

There were three in the room, including Happy. *None of their blood,* he thought swiftly. *And that means trouble!*

'No tellin' what to expect, now,' the Weasel grated. 'I didn't think you'd come—or could get here if you tried!'

'I'd like to see anybody stop me, under the circumstances,' Gentleman Jim observed. 'And I hope you haven't mistreated Happy!'

'Nah! He's even been useful,' the Weasel snarled. 'Like usual, you seem to have the devil's own luck—and we need some of that! Come in and shut the door!'

But even as he spoke, the Weasel was changing his own mind, sliding past Gentleman Jim out into the night, still clutching the gun. From across the room, lounging in a chair and busy with oiling a revolver, Big Nose Sullivan grinned in a gesture which raised his heavy moustache like the hackles of a wolf. His thatch of hair was like a Viking's mane in the glow of the coal-oil lamp.

'We're glad to see you, Jim. But there's trouble—and we may have other callers. The Weasel figured you'd be one of 'em. Naturally, we don't want them dropping in unexpected!'

Gentleman Jim shrugged, his eyes ranging the room. Happy crouched on a chair and twisted his long fingers about each other, in a way he had when distressed. He had no way of saying what must be in his mind without Sullivan hearing, so he said nothing at all. But his eyes were those of a faithful dog—troubled, but hopeful.

The next door beyond stood open, and sure instinct warned Gentleman Jim that someone was in there. Whoever had lost the blood, probably.

'You sent for me?' he suggested, pulling off his cap and helping himself to a chair.

'Yeah,' Big Nose agreed briefly. 'We had other notions in mind. But right now we're in a fix—which includes you, since you're here with us!' he added with a trace of vindictiveness.

'You boys have been up to something,' Gentleman Jim observed. 'Can't you ever be satisfied without throwing a stone at every wasps' nest you come across?'

'Ah-h, what's the world comin' to, when a man's got to keep his nose blowed?' The Weasel glided back in, snarling. 'I been ridin' the owlhoot a long time now, and I ain't no Psalm-singer!'

'Likely you'll be a rope-stretcher, before you're much older,' Big Nose retorted sharply. 'Have any trouble gettin' here,

4

Jim?'

'Why, no,' Gentleman Jim denied. 'Of course, I kind of smelled trouble—and so took my usual precautions. Are you supposed to be in a state of siege?'

'It amounts to that. But where've you been? It took you long enough to show up after we sent for you.'

'I make it a practice to come and go when and where I please,' Gentleman Jim retorted. 'As it happens, I was delayed in receiving your message, having journeyed three days' travel to the north of here. Ever hear of a town called Hangman's Coulee?'

Happy's face twisted, and he spoke for the first time.

'Sounds like a nice place,' he grunted.

'It is, Happy. You'd love it. They have paint on their houses and flowers growing around them. A most ambitious community.' He eyed the others sharply, and Big Nose answered.

'Hangman's Coulee, eh? That's almost what you'd call a coincidence. It was that town we wanted to talk about when we sent for you.'

'Indeed?'

'Yeah. How about tellin' us what news you picked up—just to see how it jibes with what we know?'

'I've no objections, certainly. I did not show myself there openly, but I did pick up

5

some interesting news. It seems, for instance, that the railroad, which has been projected for so long, is really going to build—likely before snow flies. And the point of interest is that it will either pass through Hangman's Coulee, or else go to Saddleburn, fifty miles to the north.'

'What's so interestin' about that?' the Weasel demanded.

'Just this: Hangman's Coulee is ambitious to be a metropolis. I have my doubts if it will ever be more than a pleasant town in which to live, but if they get the railroad to come their way, they are sure that they can spread like the green bay tree. On the other hand, if the rails go to Saddleburn, their town will never amount to anything. So the citizens, being solid and far-seeing, are taking practical steps to assure that the railroad's choice will be their own.'

'We heard about that,' Big Nose grunted. 'Go on.'

Gentleman Jim eyed him sharply, but complied.

'It seems that the business men, with the help of a few wealthy cattle men of the neighbourhood, are raising a hundred thousand dollars—in cash—to be turned over to the railroad to help in its construction. The only proviso being that it shall build through Hangman's Coulee.'

Happy's screwed-up face sharpened, and

6

the Weasel stared.

'A hundred thousand dollars,' Jim repeated, and the words were like falling stones.

'That sum of money interested you?' Big Nose suggested. 'In fact, knowin' you, I'll bet you've got a scheme for gettin' hold of it.'

Regretfully, Gentleman Jim shook his head.

'Unfortunately, no,' he admitted. 'I'll agree that I've been pondering the matter, but I lack a satisfactory plan for getting hold of that fund. Still, I must concede that the idea intrigues me.'

'A hundred thousand is a hell of a lot,' Big Nose agreed. 'Makes what we've been gettin' with stickups and all the rest look like chicken feed. Uh—couldn't you turn up there and say you were from the railroad, and collect?'

'I thought of that,' Gentleman Jim conceded. 'But the trouble with that is that certain representatives of the railroad have already been there. If the money is paid over, it will be to them, in person. These folks in Hangman's Coulee, as I've mentioned, are business men. And they've long since cut their eyeteeth. It would need a newer and more subtle approach.'

'Ah-h, you make me sick, talkin' like you'd swallowed a dictionary,' the Weasel

7

snarled, and shifted his wrath to Big Nose. 'What the blazes difference does it make to us now, anyway? What chance we got of ever gettin' out of here alive?'

'Since it was you who got us into this mess, you should whine,' Big Nose retorted. 'But we are in a spot, Jim. I may as well tell you that the reason we grabbed Happy and held him as a hostage was to get you to help us on this other deal. We wanted that hundred thousand—and gettin' it by force seemed to be a big order. We figured that you'd be willin' to help us out.'

Gentleman Jim eyed them coldly. He was not complimented, whatever they may have intended. He looked upon himself as a business man, though he was aware that others described him as a confidence man, and some even went so far as to add crook, or swindler.

But there was a wide gap between a man like himself, or so it seemed to him, one who lived by his wits, and plain highwaymen like Big Nose and the Weasel. He had never worked with men of their class, though he'd had a slight acquaintance with both of them. But since they had Happy as a hostage, he shrugged.

'As I told you, I was able to find no plan which seemed to be even remotely workable,' he answered.

'Maybe it don't matter—considerin' the

spot we're in,' Big Nose agreed. 'The Weasel, as usual, couldn't be satisfied to leave well enough alone. So yesterday, on his own hook, and with only Happy to help him—since they was out for a ride together—he decided to hold up the bank at Beaver Creek.'

Happy, meeting Gentleman Jim's disapproving eye, squirmed.

'I didn't like the notion,' he said defensively.

'No, Happy objected,' Big Nose agreed. 'But they went ahead and tried it, anyway.'

'And it went wrong?'

'They had fool luck at first. Everything was going all right, and they'd grabbed a couple of thousand dollars. But the Weasel wasn't satisfied with that. He had to stop to shoot the cashier—killed him in cold blood.'

'You dared implicate Happy in murder?' Gentleman Jim demanded sharply.

'Listen, a crook's a crook, in my books,' the Weasel retorted. 'Happy was holdin' the horses. As for that cashier, I recognised the dirty so-and-so. He was in that bank over at Red Pine, three years ago—and he shot my brother when him and me was stickin' that up. When I saw who he was, course I let him have it.'

'Yeah, he let him have it,' Big Nose agreed acidly. 'And the shot was heard all over town. Nobody'd known what was

9

going on, up to then. By bad luck, the two of them managed to get out—alive! Maybe because I was close enough to hear the shootin' and crazy enough to swing in and hold off pursuit till they could get started. But by that time the whole town was after us.'

'And they still are, eh?'

'Pretty much. They chased us far enough to know that we're holed up somewhere in this canyon. They're takin' their time now, knowin' we're bottled up, but if we stay much longer, they'll be bargin' in to hunt us down. They're just waitin' for enough extra men to arrive from the ranches around to have a solid line all around us. We heard 'em talkin',' he added grimly.

Gentleman Jim pondered that. He knew the lay of the land, and it could be done. There were two roads out from here—both easy to watch. And a few other trails, but not many. The cliffs took care of most of the hemming in.

'I still don't see how you got in here without them grabbin' you,' the Weasel protested now.

'Simple enough. I came down over the cliffs, near the Hogback. I had a hunch that it might be a good idea—and I follow my hunches.'

They stared at him, unbelieving.

'Over the cliffs at the Hogback?' Big Nose

repeated. 'I didn't think it could be done.'

'It was a bit tricky, at times,' Gentleman Jim agreed. 'But I'm here.'

'Tricky,' Happy breathed. 'Where one mischance could break your neck—or send you tumblin' a thousand feet!'

Sudden eagerness flared in the Weasel's eyes.

'Can we get back out, that same way?' he demanded.

'I'm afraid not,' Gentleman Jim acknowledged regretfully. 'Finding you in a state of siege, as was reasonably certain by the time I was half-way down, I was hopeful that it could be managed. But while there are a few places where a man can slide down, it would be completely out of the question to climb back up.'

The hope faded out of their faces, and again, nervous as a jaybird, the Weasel slipped back outside.

'At least, you were lucky not to get shot, with the whole town after you,' Gentleman Jim suggested.

'Shootin' could be easier'n hangin',' Happy muttered.

'Even that is a debatable point,' Gentleman Jim argued.

'Well, they shot at us plenty,' Happy protested. 'If it hadn't been for the Professor, we'd never have made it.'

'Professor?' Gentleman Jim's eyebrows

11

humped like a crawling caterpillar. 'Since when has a professor taken to aiding a bunch of holed-up highwaymen?'

'It wasn't voluntary on his part,' Big Nose explained, and chuckled. That was one of the few things which Gentleman Jim liked about this man who professed to be, in his own words, just another crook like himself. Big Nose was utterly ruthless, when such a course was required. But he combined ability with a sense of humour.

'We were close as a hound dog to a rabbit's tail to being caught,' he went on. 'They had rifles, while we had only six-guns, so they could outrange us. They shot Happy's horse from under him, then lamed mine when I gave him a hand. It looked like bones and no boothill for us, but right then, where the road turned, we come up with this professor gent, drivin' along in a covered wagon. He'd just swung out onto the main road from that side road down Lonesome, so nobody had seen the wagon. We shifted over to ride with him—fast—and sent my cayuse and the Weasel's gallopin' off ahead for them to chase, which they did. Then we cut off here—and made it.

'Time they discovered they was chasin' riderless horses, we'd reached the canyon. But they know they've got us cornered, and they'll be closin' in sure, come daylight.'

'That's about it,' Happy said. 'You got in,

12

but there ain't no way out.' He sighed. 'I'm sorry you got here just in time to get in on this, Jim. I ain't worth it, nohow. They're that riled, they'll sure string us up when they get us.'

Gentleman Jim considered this philosophically, his mind ranging the long canyon for loopholes, and finding none. The outlaws, he knew, had been living in this hide-out for several months, and if there was a way out they would long since have discovered it. From here, they had made periodic raids on the neighbouring gold camps, or had held up stages or lone travellers. More than one sample of ingrown viciousness had been displayed by the Weasel. It was that sort of thing which had now so thoroughly roused the countryside against them.

It was the fortune of war that he and Happy should be here, involved with them, at this juncture. Not that they were guilty, but Happy had been seen and recognised, and would be considered as one with the Weasel and Big Nose. Happy was known to be his, Jim's partner—and here *he* was! If caught, the posse would make no distinctions.

In fact, sometimes they did not, in any case. To hold up a man at gun-point was crude. To take a far bigger sum away by some shrewd ruse, depending on his wits, was what appealed. But there was growing evidence that it had not appealed to his victims.

The Weasel put in a nervous reappearance.

'Reckon we better be gettin' rid of the Professor an' his helper, eh?' he suggested. 'So they can't bush us or nothin' when trouble starts?'

He was fingering his gun, a restrained eagerness about him like that of a wolf pack waiting for the kill. Gentleman Jim glanced up sharply, remembering the blood.

'The Professor?' he repeated. 'Do you mean to say that he's still here? You're holding him a prisoner?'

Big Nose nodded wearily.

'They're in the next room,' he said. 'The Weasel's been wantin' to kill them, but I don't favour that, 'less we have to. Their comin' along helped us out, and they ain't raised no ruckus. The Professor's hurt—the Weasel put a bullet through his leg when we took over his wagon. Not that there was any need for that, either. They didn't offer us any resistance.'

That would account for the blood on the doorstep. Gentleman Jim stood up abruptly, and something about him caused the Weasel to shrink back, snarling in his throat. Then one of the rare ideas came to him.

'Take a look, if you like,' he growled.

14

'And either figger out a way that they'll be useful—or I'm bumpin' them out of the way! And while you're about it, you bein' such a brainy gent, figger to get us out of this mess—or I'll do the same for you!'

## CHAPTER TWO

## THE PROFESSOR

The Professor lay in one of the bunks, with his companion on a stool nearby. Both men had been listening to the conversation, but they did not seem unduly worried. The Professor was like Gentleman Jim—a tall man, dark-haired, serene of face, clean-shaven. He did not have the look of a medicine-showman. Strength and dignity were in his face, and no shadow of fear.

His companion was smaller, slighter, more on the build of Happy. Nervousness lurked in his eyes, but he seemed to draw strength from the calmness of the Professor. Gentleman Jim crossed to the bunk.

'Gentlemen,' he said, 'this is a most regrettable circumstance. I assure you that I would not have had it happen for anything, if I had known or been able to prevent it. Since my friend was more or less involved in the circumstance which later involved you

15

as well, I feel myself responsible. So you have the word of Jim Thornton that nothing further shall happen to you.'

'Listen to who's talkin'!' the Weasel snarled from the doorway behind, but the men ignored him. The Professor raised up on an elbow, regarding Gentleman Jim with frank interest.

'Jim Thornton,' he repeated. 'You will be Gentleman Jim, then? I have heard of you.'

'That's me,' Gentleman Jim agreed. 'And there'll be little of good in what you've heard, of course.'

'Hardly that, sir. Report has it that you're the most cultivated scoundrel—perhaps I should say scamp—that this country has known,' the Professor retorted. 'My name, sir, is Meader—Timothy Meader. This is my assistant, who tickles the ivory keys—John Widdicombe.'

'I'm happy to know you both,' Gentleman Jim agreed. 'I hope that your wound is not too bad, sir?'

'Just a bullet through the fleshy part of my left leg,' Meader explained. 'It bled considerably, but I should be able to get around again within a reasonable time. Did I understand you to say, sir, that you had just come from the town of Hangman's Coulee?'

'I've been up that way, yes.'

'That was our destination, as it happened,

16

when this—accident delayed us,' Meader said wryly. 'I am supposed to go there to conduct a course in civic uplift—instruction and entertainment. These stands usually run about three weeks, and I was going there by invitation. I am afraid the people there will wonder what has become of me.'

'I did hear something about a professor or something being expected there in a few days, come to think of it,' Gentleman Jim agreed. 'I took it to mean a medicine show. Would that be you?'

The Professor looked pained.

' "Medicine show" is scarcely the word, Mr. Thornton. I do not dispense spurious remedies for the gullible. Not that at all. I lecture on a variety of topics—uplifting, instructive, entertaining. I show slides with the new magic lantern, views of far and interesting places. Mr. Widdicombe performs on the organ. I might justly claim, I think, that we constitute a two man chautauqua. Our fee is modest, but commensurate with the services rendered. Medicine men are not invited to a community on such a basis.'

'My apologies,' Gentleman Jim said gravely. 'I was under a misapprehension. This is certainly a dilemma.'

'And, as you can see, their being here instead of there complicates things plenty,' Big Nose commented. 'If we have to hole

17

up here for a showdown fight, why—' he shrugged.

'We can't afford to have enemies at our backs, like I've been tellin' you,' the Weasel growled. 'Thing to do is to get rid of 'em now!'

A thoughtful look had come into Gentleman Jim's eyes. One which Happy knew of old.

'Do I understand that no one saw the wagon—or Professor Meader, on his way in here?' he demanded.

'Don't think they did,' Big Nose acknowledged. 'Why?'

'I didn't see the wagon as I came in, so I suppose it's out of sight?'

'Seemed like a good idea to keep it that way.'

'Is the team in good condition and the wagon in running order, if we should want to use them?'

'Yeah. There's a big tent in the bottom of the wagon, and a lot of other stuff.'

'The tent, which seats several hundred people, is used for our meetings; the other material consists of lantern, slides, make-up and other equipment,' Meader explained.

'I think I'll have a look,' Gentleman Jim decided. 'If you have no objections to Happy showing me?'

'Go ahead,' Big Nose agreed. 'We're in this together now. No chance of you getting

18

away.'

They went out into the night, Happy leading the way.

'Makes me feel better, just you being here,' he sighed. 'You got a scheme, Jim?'

'It all depends, Happy. But I hope so. I even begin to think so, for getting out of here.'

The Professor's team was an excellent one, two matched bays who could pull on the hills or step along on the level. But it was the wagon which interested him most, with its canvas top and the big tent, carefully folded, inside. Gentleman Jim was deeply thoughtful as he returned to the cabin.

'Have you ever visited this section of country before, Professor?' he inquired.

Meader shook his head.

'No,' he said. 'I have travelled rather widely, down through Kansas, Colorado and south. But Wyoming is all new and strange. And, er—even a trifle more turbulent than I am accustomed to.'

'But you must have some old friends or acquaintances in Hangman's Coulee, to invite you there to hold this series of lectures?'

Again Meader shook his head.

'No. I know no one there. My reputation, of course, is widely known. I have corresponded with a committee who are

19

interested in the cultural life of their community, who felt that I should come. That is all.'

Gentleman Jim pondered. Apparently, and strange as it seemed, the Professor was on the level. His only source of income appeared to be his fees or free-will offerings. It was an intriguing situation, one whose possibilities were instantly apparent to his own alert mind.

'You've got a scheme?' Big Nose suggested, echoing Happy's query.

Gentleman Jim nodded.

'I think so,' he agreed. 'One which may get us all out of this place, at least. Happy, get me some hot water, please. I'm afraid I shall have to sacrifice these sideburns and moustache to the good of the cause.'

Happy stared, knowing how proud Gentleman Jim was of his hirsute adornments. But the Weasel, as usual, missed the point.

'Now what the blazes is the point in stoppin' to shave at a time like this?' he whined petulantly.

'There is, as I recall, an old adage to the effect of helping one another. You wouldn't understand that, Weasel, but that's what we're going to do now—all of us. It is the expedient, in fact the necessary, thing to do.' Gentleman Jim was stropping his razor expertly.

'Since you say that it's impossible to get out of here alive, or to live long if we remain, you won't mind taking a chance, I'm sure. In the morning, I propose to drive out of here—on the seat of the wagon. We'll start while it's quite dark, after the moon is gone, so as to be on the road itself when daylight comes, and they first glimpse us. With your permission, Professor Meader, I shall borrow your extra suit of clothes, and endeavour to fill them creditably. Happy will ride beside me, as my assistant. As for the rest of you—' His eyes rolled over them in sardonic amusement.

'We will endeavour, Professor, to make you and Mr. Widdicombe as comfortable as possible on the floor of the wagon, padded with the tent. Like Big Nose and the Weasel, you will have to be covered by it, and, like them, it will be essential to keep silent while we pass the lines of the vigilance committee. If I am a convincing enough replica of what a cultural professor should be—then I trust that we can get safely out. All of us.'

They stared at him with something approaching awe. Happy slapped his thigh.

'By golly, it might work,' he chortled. 'That's the last thing them fellers will be lookin' for, a professor drivin' along the road, bold as brass—'

'So I trust. Or it may be that they will

21

have heard of a professor passing through. In any case, it is worth trying. They are looking for outlaws, not social uplifters.'

He observed, with some surprise, that Timothy Meader's eyes were twinkling.

'It's a good scheme,' Meader acknowledged. 'But how far do you expect to carry it?'

Gentleman Jim considered that, even as he deftly shaved off his moustache. On the one hand, there was his deep-seated resentment for the high-handed manner in which Happy had been held as a hostage for his own appearance, the notion that he, an artistic worker, should be classed in the same breath with crude performers such as Big Nose and the Weasel.

Balanced against that were the intriguing possibilities now opened up, and the equally grim fact that, like it or not, he was in with the outlaws for the present. The Weasel was trigger-happy, Big Nose Sullivan cold-blooded and ruthless. If he did not himself suggest the obvious, Big Nose's questing mind would see it for himself, with such a demonstration as he intended to put on. Half regretfully, he acknowledged to himself that it was the only way out of the trap.

'Well, now, Professor,' he said. 'I might answer you by quoting two sayings. One adjures us to take only one step at a time. The other, not to stop when you've got hold of a good thing.'

'Meaning?'

'It has occurred to me,' Gentleman Jim went on, and now his treasured sideburns were going the way of the moustache, 'that I would make a very passable professor myself. In fact, with these whiskers removed, I think that I show more than a passing resemblance to yourself, sir. We both have dark hair, a good build and, of course, a ready tongue. The people of Hangman's Coulee are expecting Timothy Meader, Professor Extraordinary. It seems to me that it would be a shame to disappoint them.'

'I've heard it said that when the devil was sick, the devil a monk would be. But that when the devil was well, the devil a monk was he!'

'And you fear that I'd be the devil of a cultural professor? I would endeavour not to bring discredit to the reputation which you have already established, I assure you.'

'But they are expecting me *and* my assistant, Mr. Widdicombe,' Meader protested. 'John plays the organ, and very well indeed. I can say, giving credit where credit is due, that a good part of my success is due to his ability. People love music. Knowing him as I do, I don't believe that he would consent to assist you in your—shall we say hoax? And how would you explain

23

his absence?'

The others had been listening, almost open-mouthed, to this conversation. The flashing minds of these two, the ease with which they seemed to understand each other, kept them a jump ahead of the outlaws. Gentleman Jim wiped the lather from his razor urbanely.

'I anticipate no trouble on that score. Happy here is of about the build of Mr. Widdicombe. And he is an old hand at tickling the ivories.'

'Who? Me?' Happy started. 'Me be a professor's assistant? I wouldn't know how.'

'You don't mean to say, Happy, that you'd let me down in time of need?' Gentleman Jim asked reproachfully.

'That ain't it, Jim. I—I just ain't got the nerve for such things, like you have—'

'And you wouldn't tell me that you are unable to play the proper music for such an occasion? The old songs, the hymns which our fathers joyed to sing? You, who pride yourself on being a virtuoso?'

'I don't rec'lect ever claimin' any such thing,' Happy denied indignantly. 'Though if they're in the book, I reckon I could play 'em. But you ain't serious?'

'I was never more so. It would be a shame to disappoint the good people of Hangman's Coulee while Professor Meader is forced to take time off for convalescing. We will find

24

some good, snug place where he can rest and recover, and Big Nose and the Weasel will remain with him to do their best as nurses to ensure his early return to good health.'

'Me?' the Weasel snorted. 'Nurse him? You're crazy! What I'd do is bump 'em off—'

Gentleman Jim turned with slow thoughtfulness. It was consideration of the Professor's condition which had been the deciding factor in this whole venture.

'At some day in the not distant future, I expect to discuss with Professor Meader just how carefully he has been looked after,' he said. 'If he gives me a favourable report, all will be fine. But should it be unfavourable—or should there be any cause for complaint on his part—in that case, Weasel, not only will I consider this other deal as null and void, but you will settle with me. I am a patient man, even long-suffering, but at times I grow annoyed. Bear that in mind.'

There was nothing threatening in words or tone, but the Weasel shrank back, his bravado curiously punctured. Timothy Meader regarded Gentleman Jim curiously.

'I really believe that you intend to try and go through with it,' he said. 'And, of course, I don't need to point out the difficulties or the risks. Giving an entertaining and at the same time a convincing lecture is not easy, but perhaps you can manage. But I am curious as to your reason for such an undertaking. To escape from this canyon—that I can understand. But the other—'

'The other has to do with what we wanted him for in the first place, and he knows it,' Big Nose interrupted. 'Gettin' hold of that hundred thousand dollars!'

Gentleman Jim looked pained, but he nodded.

'Exactly,' he agreed. 'This is strictly in line of business. As Professor Timothy Meader, with a programme for cultural and community betterment, I anticipate no serious difficulty in gaining the complete confidence of the good people of the community. And then, with the assistance of my—fellow-workers here, it should be a simple matter to get the money.'

He hesitated, eyed the Weasel appraisingly.

'So long as you fellows co-operate, I'll work at this, and we'll go fifty-fifty,' he added, still with inward distaste at the partnership. 'But if you overstep again as when you grabbed Happy—then all bets will be off. I warn you! Now let's get ready, everybody. It's about time to be moving.'

## CHAPTER THREE

# HANGMAN'S COULEE

Gentleman Jim allowed the bays to come to a stop at the crest of the hill. The canyon with its risks lay three days behind them, and no one of the vigilante posse who had stopped them had been anything but respectful to the Professor and his assistant. Timothy Meader, John Widdicombe and the two outlaws who would keep a careful watch over them until this episode was concluded, had also been left a day's journey behind.

Shifting his weight on the wagon seat, Gentleman Jim waved his whip at the scene outspread below, and addressed his companion.

'There it is, Happy,' he adjured the morose little man. 'The goal of our endeavours, the reward waiting to be plucked like an over-ripe peach hanging from a low bough. Behold the town of Hangman's Coulee!'

Happy viewed it through fretful eyes. The valley below them was not more than a quarter of a mile in width, with the hills pressing in from either side. Below them, the road wound and twisted like an

27

uncertain angleworm, requiring a half a mile to descend a third of that distance to the town. It, however, was on level ground, laid out with square streets. Even so, in the opinion of Happy, Hangman's Coulee was just another cow-town, of which already he had seen too many.

It was true that it possessed a certain neatness in the well-laid-out streets, with painted buildings and tidy flower beds missing from many another borough. But there were seven saloons which he could count, and at sight of them his melancholia deepened, like that of a thirsty traveller who, sighting deep cool water, knows in his heart that it is only a mirage.

Beyond the town, clearly visible from here, was the coulee from which it took its name—a gap in the opposite hill, out of which wound a small, sparkling stream. This watercourse twisted abruptly near the coulee's mouth, as if to avoid a giant cottonwood which stood with one great out-thrust limb. A limb worn smooth by the passage of many ropes.

'Seein' a thing like that gives me the willies,' Happy confessed.

'If you had a clear conscience, Happy, like myself, you would be untroubled in mind and reposeful in soul,' Gentleman Jim assured him, his voice a deep, rich baritone. And he clucked to the team to move ahead.

28

Happy twisted on the seat to view his companion with eyes half disparaging, half admiring. He had been down and out, and worse, when Gentleman Jim had found him and rescued him from the attentions of a mob, and since that day he had been like a faithful dog at its master's heels, almost worshipping the ground upon which the great man walked. Gentleman Jim was aware of this, and Happy knew it. But it was far from his nature to admit it openly.

Gentleman Jim Thornton, viewed now, was an eye-filling figure of a man, in his sober professional black—or Timothy Meader's black—and he looked very much like what he was not. Happy eyed the get-up dubiously. True, he had seen Gentleman Jim in the somewhat similar habiliments of a gambler on more than one occasion, but there was a difference.

'Who're you to talk about conscience?' he growled. 'You ain't on speakin' acquaintance with such.'

Gentleman Jim chuckled in vast good nature.

'Aptly put, Happy,' he concluded. '*Touché*, as the French would say, or so I've been told. But don't be so dolorous. No one is going to be looking for Gentleman Jim Thornton or Happy Brant in Hangman's Coulee, or in such guise as we come. They are expecting Professor Timothy Meader, social uplifter, and his organ master, John Widdicombe. As such we are arriving. Try and look human, if you can't look pleasant. And remember—not even one snort of liquor! You know your weakness!'

'And you tell me to look pleasant!' Happy sighed. He squirmed on the wagon seat like a small boy. 'I got a feelin' that we're makin' fools of ourselves,' he added resignedly. 'Likely we'll finish up, swingin' from that Hangman's Tree ourselves.'

'At least, we would be following in the line of many distinguished predecessors.' Gentleman Jim smiled. 'And now forget such things. From now on I am Professor Timothy Meader, while you are John Widdicombe, master of the ivory keys.'

'I can play 'em, even for hymns, if I don't forget where I am and go thinkin' I'm poundin' a piano in a beer parlour,' Happy grumbled, and subsided.

But if his mind was ill at ease, that was only a habitual condition, and it did not apply to Gentleman Jim. He was completely cool, alert, and with the pleasant determination, having decided upon a course, to enjoy the adventure to the utmost, as he did with everything. Happy had been correct in his judgment. Gentleman Jim had no conscience. Or, if so, it had so long been pushed aside and neglected, that it had ceased to trouble him.

This enterprise was a gamble, of course, as was everything which the two of them tried. A gamble, with the ever-present risk that they might indeed adorn the branches of Hangman's Tree if anything went wrong. But this adventure had a flavour all its own, and if risks were present, they were no bigger than usual. Likewise, the stakes were high.

Ever since he had visited this town, keeping carefully out of sight, and had heard of that hundred thousand dollars, Gentleman Jim had been racking his brains for a plan to get it. Opportunity had knocked in a guise which most men might not have recognized, but it suited him.

The one fly in his ointment was the association and potential partnership with a pair of real outlaws. That was forced by necessity, but he didn't like it. Still, it was his pride, not his conscience, which was hurt.

Hangman's Coulee was, on the map, just another cow-town—though most maps ignored it entirely. But at heart it was far more than that. Like himself, it had ambitions. It yearned to be respectable, progressive, and to gain a place for itself on all maps.

It was certain that the money would be raised. They had discussed plans for getting hold of it at some length with Big Nose.

31

Happy had still been opposed to the whole scheme on the grounds that it was too risky.

'A hundred thousand iron men—always supposin' that they raise 'em—ain't goin' to be easy to grab off,' he had argued. 'They're gettin' that money by squeezin' it out of their own pocketbooks. Like blood. And they'll be guardin' it mighty careful. Tryin' to get it'll be a short cut to Boothill.'

'But this is a different sort of a gamble,' Gentleman Jim had pointed out.

'Yeah. And suppose that somebody remembers you—as a gambler? Or worse? The law's right anxious to get its hands on Gentleman Jim Thornton. What does them dodgers say? Highwayman, robber, wanted for murder—'

Gentleman Jim had turned a suddenly bleak eye on his diminutive partner at that juncture, and the words had frozen on Happy's lips.

'I've never killed a man in my life, and you know it,' he reminded sharply. 'And I never will!'

'Sure, Jim, we know that,' Big Nose had hastened to the rescue. 'But the law thinks you have, same as it thinks a lot of other things about you, just on general principles. And it'd like to hang you on them principles, if nothing else.'

'They won't be looking for Gentleman Jim in the guise of a professor,' Gentleman

Jim had retorted confidently. 'By the time the full sum of money is collected, everyone will know me, and have confidence in me, as their natural leader and friend. Then you will come along, and the actual job of getting the money should be a simple matter.'

'It might work,' Big Nose had conceded. 'If you can get away with your end of it. But do you think that you're cut out to do this lecturin' and all?'

'Have you ever heard of me failing in any role I ever tried?'

'You're a mighty good actor, and a smooth worker,' Big Nose had agreed dubiously. 'That's why I thought of you for this job in the first place, when I saw me and the Weasel couldn't work it alone. But you helped us out of a tight spot, Jim, and I kind of got to thinkin'. But this professorin' business strikes me as bein' a lot diff'rent. It's a long way outside your field.'

'I'll handle it,' Gentleman Jim said confidently.

*       *       *

Now they were rattling down the last slope into town, and to the square at the middle. This was flanked on one side by the Cattleman's Saloon, with the Silver Dollar Drink Emporium opposite. Tall trees stood

33

in the centre, with a watering trough and hitch rail, and into the former the thirsty horses dipped grateful muzzles.

By now a crowd was beginning to collect—a few cowboys, and a scattering of the townspeople. Among them came a broad-shouldered, thin-waisted man of about Gentleman Jim's own age—slightly short of thirty. Like Jim, he was dressed in broadcloth, though this was a business suit. He had a frankly welcoming smile on his face, and other, older men followed at his heels.

'You're Professor Meader, of course,' he declared, thrusting out his hand. 'Welcome to our town! We're delighted to have you with us. I am John Gilson. Permit me to introduce my friends.'

He did so, while Happy stared in a half-daze. Gilson, he knew, was the banker, in charge of the money being raised for the railroad. He was also, it appeared, one of the prime movers in this desire to bring uplift to the town.

Since they were arriving as scheduled, with the little organ and the big tent in the wagon, no one seemed to have any suspicion that they might not be as represented. Their welcome was warmly enthusiastic, and Happy, forgetting a bit of his apprehension, was beginning to warm when he suddenly froze again.

Another man was pushing through the crowd toward them. And this man wore a sheriff's star.

He would never, Happy knew, be wholly at ease in the presence of the law. Memory of his last escapade, into which he had been dragged by the Weasel, increased his apprehension. And this young fellow behind the badge had a coldly businesslike look which was disconcerting.

Where others had accepted Gentleman Jim on sight and without question, Happy had a chill foreboding that this law dog was not so confiding. He halted, allowing his gaze to rake across the face of the Professor, then shifting it to Happy, and under the probe of those light blue eyes, the little man squirmed. If ever he had seen suspicion in a man's face, it was in Sheriff Paul Hoffman's.

Happy knew Gentleman Jim well enough to be sure that he saw the suspicion. But he gave no indication of unease. His greeting for the sheriff was as hearty, his handclasp as warm, as for any of the others. The fact that his likeness, in somewhat altered guise, might now be upon one or many dodgers reposing in the sheriff's desk, did not trouble him.

'Sheriff Hoffman? This is a pleasure. And I sincerely trust that our efforts here, during the next few weeks, will be so fruitful that when we have finished, there will be little left for you to do, beyond purely routine duties.'

'I'm afraid that day is a long way off, in this community,' the sheriff said, and his tone was short.

'There are great possibilities in even the worst of us,' Gentleman Jim pronounced. 'All that is required is that they be stirred, wakened. It can be done.'

The sheriff made no answer, but Happy saw a flicker of doubt in his eyes. Not enough to allow him to breathe easily, however. He glanced toward that grim giant of a tree, there at the edge of the coulee, which had given this town its name, and he shivered. Of all the crazy notions which Gentleman Jim had ever had, this was the worst.

Happy had nourished a brief hope that, seeing how the wind blew, Gentleman Jim would lose no time in finding an excuse and leaving town. Even a poor excuse would be better than none, and he'd sooner face Big Nose and the Weasel than this set-up. But he heard the banker inviting them to make his house their home while they remained in town, and Gentleman Jim accepting. Happy jerked his moody gaze away from the distant tree. While they were eating supper, the sheriff would be thumbing through his dodgers again, to refresh his memory. And then—

It was bad. Bad for bad men trying to act like good ones, Happy thought confusedly. And then, as they entered the banker's house and their hostess came forward to greet them, he had a despairing conviction that all was lost.

## CHAPTER FOUR

# THE TENT MEETING

Gentleman Jim had been as swiftly aware as Happy of that look in the eyes of the sheriff. He had recognized it as a danger signal, but, unlike his more timid partner, he was not much worried. He had known from the start that this job, like all the work in which they specialized, was a gamble, and he loved that part of it.

But he had been quick to sense something more—proof of what the professor had claimed, that he had built a reputation which meant something. It came to Gentleman Jim that Meader had been in earnest, that he might actually be entitled to his title and have a string of degrees after his name. This was no medicine-show affair.

That made a lot of difference. And since the sheriff had not immediately arrested them, it was plain that he had his doubts. The best way would be to play the game through and decrease those doubts until by that process they were finally removed.

When Maita Gilson came forward to greet him, Gentleman Jim temporarily lost his breath and the power of speech. Maita was good to look at, but her beauty went deeper than the surface. It was a spirit which shone through like a lamp in a dark room, a sort of breathless singing quality that set her apart. Happy had been right in his guess. Gentleman Jim was smitten.

Not because of her conversation. Never had he met a woman who had less to say. She acknowledged the introduction, adding a word of welcome, and instructed her brother to show them to their room, while she put supper on the table. Being a guest here in the banker's house was final proof that Professor Meader was accepted as a man of consequence. Otherwise, save for brief answers while the meal progressed, Maita did not have a word to say. Happy viewed her in surprise. He hadn't known that women like that existed.

But if she was silent, John Gilson talked fluently, and Gentleman Jim, as always, matched him.

'We've got scores of volunteers, Professor,' Gilson explained. 'With their help, we'll have your tent up in a jiffy, then

38

move in logs and place planks across them for seats. People are interested, and I anticipate a good crowd. Everything will be ready for the meeting this evening.'

'I certainly appreciate such fine co-operation,' Gentleman Jim agreed warmly. And afterward, while Happy struggled with a fresh set of qualms, he dissipated them by directing how the big tent should be raised, and assisting in the job, as skilfully as though he had done such a task every day for years. Belatedly, Happy remembered hearing that, in his boyhood, Gentleman Jim had travelled for a while with a circus.

The tent was raised at the edge of town, beside the clear waters of the creek, not far from the spectre of the hanging tree. Gentleman Jim kept a sharp eye on his helper, knowing Happy's weakness for a bit of alcoholic stimulant, but he saw that Happy was far too frightened to risk any indulgence now. If trouble broke, he wanted a clear head and a pair of legs which would carry him places.

Now that they were actually here, Gentleman Jim had to admit that this was probably the most fantastic of all the schemes that he had ever dreamed up. After all, though he could sing and talk fluently, could he give an entertaining address which was also scholarly and meaningful? A lot of these people had come from other parts of the country, and they had had experience with lecturers of ability. How could he hope to fool them? And, remembering Maita Gilson, the warm, friendly look that she had given him, he wondered for a moment if he wanted to.

This was June, and it would be a long evening. Already, people were beginning to come in from the country, in wagons and buggies and on horseback, men and women and children. The majority of them were heading for the big tent, dressed in their best, so that the town was beginning to take on almost a holiday appearance.

A lot of people had come out of curiosity, others with the hope of being entertained. He had no fears of any of them. But there would be some who wanted something beyond that, and those he knew he could not fool. He had to give them something, or they, and the sheriff as well, would know him for an impostor.

Happy's music, at the start, a little community singing, and a set of the lantern slides once it grew dark, would pretty well take care of the entertainment. Which left a lot of time in between. There was, he decided, just one way to do it. When you had a job to do, the idea was to throw yourself into it, heart and soul—to believe the part you were playing. Always he had done it that way, and it made for sincerity. But what would he talk about?

Unexpectedly, Maita Gilson supplied the answer.

'I've heard that you are a powerful temperance lecturer, Professor,' she said. 'And a great foe of gambling. That's what we need here. I don't mean that I want to close all the saloons and make this a bone-dry town, or anything like that. That would be impossible, of course, and impractical as well. But the way some things are conducted now—so wide open and flagrantly—we need a housecleaning, a change of heart.'

Gentleman Jim did not bat an eye. For an instant some of his own past flashed in mental review, but he dismissed it without a tremor. His answer came promptly.

'That's what I hope to do, Miss Gilson. What I'll be talking about tonight, and on other occasions before we're through here.'

Happy glanced sharply at him, startled, then crossed to the organ. The big tent was nearly full, and Gentleman Jim stood to lead in singing. 'Silver Threads Among the Gold.' 'Loch Lomond.' 'Rock of Ages.' One after another, for half an hour. They went well. Then, as the last song ended, Gentleman Jim felt a moment of panic. Then it passed, and he leaned forward.

'Friends,' he said quietly. 'I have come

41

here, and I know that you are here too, for one purpose—that we all may be better, mentally, and in all other ways, for this meeting of minds. We might spend all our time in light entertainment, or in singing. Or in deep discussion of those fundamentals which affect the lives of all of us. I think that a judicious mingling of all will be better. My hope is that we'll all get what we really want, out of these meetings.'

*That sounds good*, Happy reflected dourly. *Only it can't be done! Not with us wantin' that hundred thousand bucks, the sheriff wantin' us and the crowd wantin' what we ain't got to give!*

But even Happy was beginning to have his doubts as Gentleman Jim really got under way. He could fairly talk a bird off a tree, and he was doing it now. Entertainingly, but straight from the shoulder. His theme, as he had announced it, was crooks. And he'd ought to know a lot about them, Happy reflected.

What he was really doing was laying the foundation for a better town—one in which all good citizens could take pride, but in which flagrant lawlessness would not be allowed to flourish. That was what Maita had suggested, and he was responding. So was the crowd as they listened to him.

In the middle of the discourse, a gunshot sounded on the night, from some distance away. It was followed by a wild yippee from the throats of several men, and more guns serenaded the stars. Gentleman Jim paused, but the sounds were drawing nearer as fast as running horses could bring them. Heading straight for the tent.

A moment later fully a score of men were milling outside, whooping it up and discharging their guns wildly into the air. After a moment they began to circle the tent. While such pandemonium continued, there was no chance to go on talking. Gentleman Jim relaxed, waiting. The boys wanted their fun.

This, he supposed, was their way of welcoming the Professor to Hangman's Coulee. After a few minutes of it they'd go away, heading for the saloons to lubricate their stretched tonsils. On future evenings they might even venture here to listen and to imbibe a little culture.

But it was soon clear that they were not going away. Happy was the first to sense it, to guess that others had heard of the Professor's intention of putting a curb on the town and a bit in its mouth, and that they might not like it. The way to break that sort of thing up, they figured, was to do it before it got well started.

All at once a horseman came surging in at the rear of the tent, where the canvas was tied back to make a doorway. Behind him, still yelling and shooting, came the others.

There was a space six to eight feet wide around the outside of the seats, but still within the canvas confines. Now the guns were blasting at the tent top, the riders spurring to a gallop around and around. Faces lost their colour as the audience drew back and watched. Some of the women and children were close to panic.

Gentleman Jim's face drew tight. This matter of a few of the boys having fun was one thing, and he did not disapprove of it. But not only were they carrying the joke too far, but it looked to him also like something more than fun. The purpose seemed to be to intimidate and to break up this meeting.

Now they had made a couple of complete circles inside the tent. Instead of heading back out again, they were starting on a third, their shooting becoming more indiscriminate.

Someone gasped as the Professor stepped abruptly down from behind the speaker's stand, straight into the path of the plunging cayuses. There was a moment of confused mêlée, then the horses were sliding to a halt. Gentleman Jim had grabbed the bridle rein of the lead horse, close up to the bit, jerking it to a stop. With his other hand he had the rider by the arm, and it all looked part of an act, it worked so smoothly. The next moment he had pulled the rider completely

44

out of the saddle, onto his feet in front of him.

Expertly he swung the riderless cayuse sidewise, blocking the others, forcing them to stop in a cloud of dust. Up to now he had still more than half supposed that this was intended for fun, which had gotten out of hand. But he saw now that he had hold of a man even bigger than himself, and there was no trace of humour or fun-seeking in those agate-hard eyes, that leathery jaw. Something quite the contrary.

'When you come here seeking personal instruction,' Gentleman Jim said, 'remember to act like a gentleman. Since you forgot, turn around and apologize to the crowd—*on your knees!*'

## CHAPTER FIVE

## CARDS ON THE TABLE

The other riders were stopped now, their winded cayuses more than willing to stand. All were watching, like the audience. Here was the Professor's first test. He had issued a challenge and an ultimatum, but could he make it stick? The thin-lipped cowboy's retort was savagely contemptuous.

'Go to hell, word-shark!'

45

What he had expected, Gentleman Jim guessed was that this embodiment of the erudite would cringe back, or, if prepared to back his bluff, that he'd hit him at that remark. Instead, there was a hand on his collar, twisting the shirt like a closing noose, spinning him down. Gentleman Jim's other hand was on his right arm, bending it back in a painful grip, till all the fight went out of him. For the cowboy knew with a dire sense of certainty that if he resisted the bone would snap.

Then he was down on his knees, helpless even to struggle. Complete silence had descended across the big tent, save for the impatient pawing of a horse. An aching silence, by contrast with the uproar which had prevailed.

'I've seen horses that I liked better than some men,' Gentleman Jim said quietly. 'Also some that are considerably more intelligent. Still and all, I doubt if they'd enjoy the lecture, so if you boys will get them back outside, the rest of us will be obliged. You're welcome to come back in by yourselves. Only you don't have to go to such lengths to advertise that you're in need of what we might describe as the social graces. We all feel the need and recognize the room for improvement in ourselves, individually and collectively. That's why we're here.'

He released his grip on the ringleader, stepped back. Slowly, bewilderment large on his face, the other man got to his feet. He eyed the Professor uncertainly, but the meanness had gone out of his own. This word-shark was quite a man, and he had made an impression. The cowboy turned and led his own horse outside, the others following.

'As I was saying,' Gentleman Jim went on, 'the life of a community can only be as good as its sore spot, just as a man with a boil on the back of his neck cannot get his thoughts on loftier subjects. For the good of all concerned, we must remove the sore spot—restore it to a state of health.'

He had his audience with him now. Those who had come intending to ridicule, had been caught by the way he had handled Bill Bender. It took a man to do that, as plenty would have been ready to attest. Gentleman Jim's voice flowed on, deepening, gripping. Happy looked at him, awed, more than a little disturbed. It was bewildering, but he *was* the Professor!

Finally it was over, and the people were crowding up to shake his hand, congratulating themselves and him. They had liked it, and they liked him. The lantern slides, following that talk, had been almost an anti-climax.

The sheriff was there, and there was a

47

puzzled, doubtful look on his face. Happy saw Maita Gilson come up, and her eyes held a light that reminded him of the stars.

'Professor Meader,' she said, 'that was wonderful. You made us think as individuals, but collectively—a sort of united mind. I—I can't quite express it, I haven't the words like you have, but I know that we made no mistake in getting you here!'

Praise was pleasant, particularly when coming from such a source. But now that the spell of his own words was broken, Gentleman Jim was troubled. One part was going as he had planned it—he was being accepted here. But certainly the thought of organizing and leading a crusade had been farthest from his mind. What did he know about such matters—except from the other side of the fence?

He fought down a momentary feeling of panic, such as a trapped animal must experience when it finds there is no give to the steel jaws. After all, this was just another job, with one real goal in mind. Why should he worry about other aspects, or about it getting beyond his control?

There were certain elements here which he had not counted on. For one, their being invited to stay with the Gilsons. That was a real courtesy, and to be accepted as such. But it was both pleasant and embarrassing.

48

Under this arrangement it was only natural, following the lecture, to walk home with the Gilsons. He found himself beside Maita, while Happy went ahead with her brother. Their course took them past the now brilliantly lit saloons.

'It will take a lot—a lot of words, and probably more than that, to make any impression on the—on those who are back of what goes on around here,' Maita said, with a gesture toward the buildings. 'But I do hope—'

She halted abruptly as a man stepped out to the sidewalk, almost directly in front of them. As though he had been waiting for them, watching as they approached. He was doffing his hat to them, but deliberately blocking their way.

Gentleman Jim catalogued him swiftly as one of the proprietors here. A tall man, he was also portly, but he carried his weight easily. His was a strong face, that of a man who would brook little opposition.

*And here's the real reason why I—why the Professor—was asked to come here*, Gentleman Jim thought, in a swift flash of intuition. *There's more here than appears on the surface—a lot more!*

'Good evening, Miss Maita,' he greeted, and glanced inquiringly, arrogantly, over Gentleman Jim. 'I see that you've kept your word.'

Maita's eyes were level, a little brighter than usual, but whether with anger or some other emotion, Gentleman Jim was not quite sure.

'I always keep my word, Deal Hathaway,' she answered. 'Professor Meader, Mr. Hathaway here is proprietor of the Cattleman's Saloon. I told him that we were going to bring a man to town who would make him clean up the sort of place he runs.'

'It's a shame that we must always be fighting, Maita,' Hathaway observed. 'And I call you to witness, Professor, that it's not of my desire.' He did not offer to shake hands. 'You had a good crowd tonight,' he added, and his moustache lifted sardonically. 'I'm serving refreshments to many of them now. I suppose the other was a dry business.'

Behind Maita's head he jerked his own in a gesture. Gentleman Jim understood it, and presently, having left Maita at her door, he returned to find the saloon-man waiting for him. Hathaway was picking his teeth with a gold toothpick.

'Since you're here, I'd like to have a talk with you, Professor,' he said directly. 'Would my office contaminate you?'

'I've probably been in worse places,' Gentleman Jim returned, and followed him into the saloon and so down to his office. Not until the door had closed behind them did Hathaway speak again.

'I've a double purpose in asking you to come here tonight, Professor,' he confessed and smiled wryly. 'For once, I'm in an unusual position—not knowing quite what I want to do.'

'I'd judge that wouldn't happen often,' Gentleman Jim agreed, studying the strong jaw, the steely grey eyes of the man.

'You're right,' Hathaway agreed. 'I usually know exactly what I want to do and how to go about getting it. But your coming here has brought me to a crossroads. After listening to the reports of your meeting tonight, I know that. Maybe I'm a fool to discuss it with you—I wouldn't even know about that.' He made a disarming gesture, and there was something likcable about the man in that moment.

'You still haven't told me anything,' Gentleman Jim reminded him. 'Nor do you have to, you know.'

'But that's the devil of it; I do. I've got to know—about some things, at least, as to where I stand. The only way that I can see is to talk it over with someone, and you seem to be the logical man for that. The Gilsons have been prime movers in getting you here, and you know what they want you for. To change me—make me over, or to drive me out. Perhaps you don't understand that too well, but you will—if you stay here

51

long. I'm considered the boil on the neck, as you call it. I'm not sure which they would prefer—to drive me out, or to change me. Sometimes I think one thing—and then I'm just as certain that I'm a fool.'

He stared out of the window at the distant stars a moment, went on grimly.

'It's no secret in this town—not to her, nor to the populace at large—that I've been courting Maita Gilson for the last half-year.'

Gentleman Jim waited. He was suddenly tense inside, conscious of an interest, even a resentment, at the words of the saloon-keeper. Almost of a feeling of jealousy. But his well-schooled face gave no indication of it.

'I suppose you're surprised at that,' Hathaway went on. 'In view of the rest. But, while they don't like my business—or the way I do some things—I think they do like me—more or less.'

Still Gentleman Jim waited. Hathaway gave him a sharp glance.

'As I say, your coming to town sort of brings a showdown,' he grunted. 'I love her—I'd do anything to win her—almost.' He fell silent a moment, placing the tips of his fingers together with an abstracted interest. 'I've never considered myself a hypocrite,' he added quietly. 'At least, not till lately.'

*Here it is*, Gentleman Jim thought, his

mind bridging gaps. *She's told him off—and he's not the kind of man to take kindly to currying!*

'She knows my business and what I stand for,' Hathaway added explosively. 'I've always been open about it. I've thought I could overcome her scruples. Today I have my doubts.'

'Today you have doubts about yourself,' Gentleman Jim suggested.

'Maybe that's it. I'm not sure. There's one thing I could do, of course—attend your lectures, get a civic conscience—that's what you call it, isn't it?—and become a tame monkey on a leash. At least to the extent of making some changes. That would please her.'

'But it wouldn't please you.'

He made it as a simple statement of fact, and Hathaway looked at him shrewdly.

'For a professor, you have more sense than I gave you credit for,' he conceded. 'I didn't take your coming seriously, until tonight. I figured you as a sort of medicine-man, here to get some easy pickings. Knowing the Gilsons, I should have known better. And the devil of it is that you're right. I could change, but I wouldn't feel right. Whatever else I've been, and am, I don't consider myself a hypocrite. I don't believe in any of that sort of thing—the sort that leads to churches coming to town, for instance. I couldn't respect myself if I took that way out of it. I doubt if she would respect me, either.'

Gentleman Jim understood—better than Hathaway suspected. Deal Hathaway was a gambler, and a hard man. He loved Maita Gilson, probably as much as it was possible for a man of his nature to love anything not made with his own hands, anything save himself.

That was the rub. Hathaway was the sort of man with whom his business came first, and always would. A woman would have her place in his life, but it must not be one which would interfere with things as he had planned them. In a wife, he would want a woman who could keep his house, who would wear clothes well and beyond that she must not go. No woman could dominate him, not even to the extent of influencing him in such a decision as this. That was what bothered him, what he was striving to get straight in his own mind.

'Your trouble,' Gentleman Jim suggested, 'is that you've picked the wrong kind of woman, Hathaway. I infer that you've clashed about certain aspects of your business. My judgment is that she is just as strong in her opinions as you are in yours. That would mean that a change must be made somewhere, a compromise reached. You want what you want, which happens to be to run your affairs as you please, and still have her. You're not willing to pay the necessary price to satisfy her.'

Hathaway had trimmed and lit a cigar, without offering one to Gentleman Jim. Now he smoked for a minute in silence. Finally he nodded.

'Maybe that's it,' he agreed. 'I thought I could get this straightened out by talking about it. But aren't you advising me to give up all this—to turn over a new leaf and all that sort of thing?'

Gentleman Jim shrugged.

'Why should I?' he asked. 'I'm no preacher. Maybe that's what you need, to listen to one—though I doubt it. But you wouldn't turn that leaf until you have a change of heart. If you get that, sure. But it will take something bigger even than Maita Gilson in your life to bring that about.'

'Thanks, Professor, for straightening me out. You have got sense. And since I know, as you're trying to tell me, that there's nothing else will ever bulk as big as she does, I won't change. There's an old saying that a man should stick to his own game. I will.'

'In that case, I may as well be going.'

'No, sit still. Maybe we can talk business.'

'I understood you before. Now I don't.'

'You should. You're no fool. I've thought all along that I could win her by showing

55

her that my way works. I still think so. The only thing that can spoil it is you—and this civic uplift stuff. Folks say that you gave them a real talk tonight. That, and the way you handled trouble, made quite an impression. Two or three were blubbering into their beer. I can wash out all that with whisky in a few days—providing it doesn't happen too often.'

'There's some things whisky won't wash out, Hathaway.'

'That's what I'm driving at. I've heard preachers say, back when I was a boy, that it takes blood—and maybe it does. But when I talk about blood, I mean different from what they do, and I'd prefer that it needn't come to that here.'

He made the threat calmly, never batting an eye.

'Now take a man like you, Professor. You've got ability and a chance for a big future, if you were in the right place and with the right set-up—instead of lecturing in jay-towns like this for the collection—chicken feed. If you had a real start, to go somewhere and build up—money enough not to worry while you were getting started—you could do almost anything you wanted to. Eh?'

'It sounds interesting.'

'Well, it can be. Pull out of here—say in a week. You can stay that long to make it look

56

right. Only kind of taper off on your talks as you go along, so that everybody will see that the whole notion has been a failure. Then pull out—and you can have the cash that you need in your pocket.'

It was the direct sort of a bribe that Gentleman Jim had expected of such a man. Curiously, he found himself bewildered by his own reaction. Here was a perfect set-up. A week here would be long enough, if he worked it right. And he could leave with an extra cash dividend of no mean proportions, merely for the taking.

Under such circumstances, it was odd that he should feel anger at the proposition, a mounting indignation. Which was exactly the way it was affecting him. He realized that Maita had done that to him, knew it for a danger signal. But, stubbornly, he shook his head.

'I'm afraid we can't do business, Hathaway,' he said. 'Not on those terms.'

'I haven't named my price. Shall we say five thousand?'

'It's generous—if I was interested.'

Hathaway shook his head, almost regretfully. But he did not argue nor raise his price.

'I'm afraid you don't understand, Professor,' he protested. 'There's something about you that I rather like. Which is strange, considering that you're here to buck me. But that's the way of it. So I don't want to have to play rough. This other way would be so much better, all round.'

Gentleman Jim stood up.

'Sorry, Hathaway,' he said. 'But if we do business, it will have to be on my terms—over at my place. And if you ever want to stand a chance with Miss Gilson—I'm afraid that's your only chance, too.'

'I'm sorry, too,' Hathaway retorted. 'I hope you understand, Meader. If I can't get what I want one way, I take another. And I play rough—when I have to.'

## CHAPTER SIX

# THE SECOND MEETING

The Gilsons were among the more prosperous settlers of the town. Since John Gilson was the banker, that was to be expected. Their place was roomy and comfortable, with a homey atmosphere which Gentleman Jim had rarely encountered in his years of knocking around. An atmosphere which made Happy vaguely uneasy.

'We'd ought to get out of here,' he protested, the next morning. 'This'll spoil

58

us.'

'How do you mean?' Gentleman Jim yawned. 'It's very comfortable.'

'Sure. Too rich for our blood, is what I mean. Look. Lace curtains, flowers in pots, a rug on the floor and all that sort of thing. The other was bad enough, but I didn't bargain for this. It's too much.'

Despite her position as the banker's sister, Maita did all her own housework. That she was an excellent cook and an efficient housekeeper had already been demonstrated. Now, breakfast over, Gentleman Jim strolled out to the kitchen to find her baking, arms white with flour, the tea kettle singing on the stove, a yellow canary echoing it from its cage in a shaft of sunlight. She looked very beautiful and domestic, with a round little face almost guilelessly innocent. But her first question, as she looked up, was disconcerting.

'What did Deal Hathaway want last night?'

It was on the tip of his tongue to tell her the truth—that Hathaway wanted him to get out of town. Then he checked. Hathaway had been frank in admitting that he wanted to marry this woman. It wouldn't be quite fair to strike back at him in such a fashion.

'He seemed interested in what we are trying to do—though not from quite the angle that might be desired,' Gentleman Jim explained. 'He appears to be a forthright sort.'

'Yes,' Maita agreed. 'But he and his kind have got to go—one way or another.' She kneaded a loaf into shape, placed it in a bread pan and slipped the pan into the oven alongside several others. 'Hangman's Coulee was a name that fitted this town, a year or two ago. It still does. But it won't—six months from now. There will be a new and better name—and a new and better town.'

She said it with quiet conviction, and he believed her. The railroad was one step in that building and regeneration. His own coming—or that of the man they believed him to be—was another step, equally vital in the eyes of such men as her brother, who took a long look into the future, of such women as herself. Where Deal Hathaway sought only to perpetuate the old, at his own profit, they strove to build up.

Theirs was foresight. One sort of profit could be won only from a new, raw community. Once it became stable that would be gone.

It was a new notion, though he knew that it ought not to have been. It would have been perfectly natural to Timothy Meader. To him, it was just one more reason for a growing unease of mind which he could not shake off. Maybe Happy had been right, and they had been fools to come here in the first place. For he too had belonged to that raw fringe. What else had he ever known?

He was invited to address the business men of the town at noon, in the biggest restaurant. The cattle men who took an interest in Hangman's Coulee, who were putting up some of the money being raised for the railroad, would be there as well. He shaved carefully, prepared to play his part. John Gilson introduced him, and there were forty men waiting for what he had to say. Deal Hathaway was one of them.

Among the group was the sheriff, his eyes still suspicious, though he had made no change in his attitude from the day before. It was as though he was watchfully waiting. He was seated beside Hathaway, and Gentleman Jim had learned that the saloon man had put up five thousand dollars toward the railroad. Gentleman Jim stood up.

'A man,' he said quietly, 'can be his own worst enemy—and frequently is. The same thing can apply to a group of men.'

They were silent, interested but puzzled. He went on.

'There are some here who want the railroad to come to town, because it will mean one thing to them. Others among you want it to come for quite another purpose. The business that it brings, the hard-fighting, hard-drinking, hard-gambling men who always accompany a construction crew, and the horde of parasites who always hang upon the fringes, preying upon them—that business will be welcomed too, by some of you here. But it will be of quite a different nature than the benefits which others of you envision.'

He saw the startled glances being exchanged, and Hathaway's eyes had grown cold.

'That, of course, is just a passing phase, and the benefits, in the long run, will undoubtedly exceed the temporary ills. But some of you see beyond the railroad. Some of you want more than a line of steel, or houses in which to take shelter from the hot sun of summer or the snows of winter. You wish to build homes in an atmosphere no longer chill with the rawness of life as you have had to face it. You want a school, a church, a decent place in which to raise your families, free from such influences as I have just alluded to.

'Which is where you differ one from another. I have no intention of criticizing, or of working to stir up strife. Co-operation is what is needed. But to get what you want, a solid foundation must be laid, in this as in anything else. Otherwise you're apt to get what you don't want.'

He paused a moment, went on

deliberately.

'I would counsel you who have a long-range plan for this community, to look first to your own committee and see that you are not working at cross-purposes, that your goal is a common one. Otherwise, you may get nowhere. More than one enterprise has made a good beginning, only to be twisted to the selfish ends of some one clever but unscrupulous man. I wouldn't want to see that happen here.'

He sat down, amid a thoughtful silence. There was no polite applause, but the mask-like face of Hathaway had drawn tighter. Well, Hathaway had said that he played rough. There was more than one way of playing rough, if he wanted it that way.

It had been a good move on his part, Gentleman Jim discovered, and was ironically amused. He had come here to build up confidence in himself in the minds of the substantial citizens, and nothing could have worked better than those few words. They understood him, and men like Gilson would take steps to see that Deal Hathaway did not profit too much at their expense.

'I'd heard tell that you were a fighter, when you got into anything, Professor,' the banker commented, once they were out on the street again. 'Seems there's no mistake about that. Do you pack a gun?'

63

The abrupt question was a little startling. Gentleman Jim shook his head.

'Why, no,' he said. 'It hardly seems compatible with my work.'

'It might be a good idea if you did,' Gilson suggested thoughtfully. 'You may need it. We didn't get you here to precipitate a showdown, exactly, but it looks as though we'll have it. On the whole, it's probably a good thing.'

Happy, for one, did not seem to share the banker's optimism, though he did hold to the same opinion. He waxed sarcastic, back in their room.

'What's come over you, Jim?' he demanded. 'Sure, I know you're the Professor here, and all that sort of thing. But I can't picture you as leadin' a crusade—and anyway, what's it goin' to get us, except in bad? Hathaway, he'd have been on our side if we'd given him a chance.'

Gentleman Jim shook his head soberly.

'You've got me, Happy,' he confessed. 'I guess I'm a better actor than I know, at playing a part. I seem to be saying and doing a lot of things that surprise me as much as they do you.'

Happy eyed him anxiously.

'You never talked nor acted this way before,' he said. 'We better get out of town, soon as it gets dark. It'll be cheap at the price, as we don't owe anything to Big Nose or the Weasel.' He waited a moment, watching his companion, sighed. 'Oh, well,' he added resignedly. 'There's one good thing about it. They can't lynch a man but once.'

To Gentleman Jim's surprise, he was stopped on the street by Bill Bender, the man who had led the cowboys in their invasion of the tent the night before. He seemed a changed man by the light of day, sober-faced and regretful.

'I want to apologize for last night, Professor,' he said. 'I guess I was kinda drunk. I—the rest of the boys was just out to have some fun. But me—I knew better. I'd been slipped a month's wages to bust up yore meetin'.' He straightened his shoulders. 'I'm payin' that money back—now. But I wanted you to know.'

*And that,* Gentleman Jim reflected, *was before Hathaway and I confabbed!*

The big tent had been comfortably filled on the first evening. Tonight it was crowded. This Professor was more than just an ordinary medicine man, as he had demonstrated. More to the point, the news, though never more than whispered, was all around the town. The Professor had tangled with Deal Hathaway, and Hathaway would not take such an affront lying down.

Happy played, and Gentleman Jim led

the singing again. There was something about music. It did things to you. Or maybe it was Maita Gilson's eyes, bright on his face.

For a few minutes he told funny stories, to set them to laughing. Then, remembering something that he had once seen as a boy, he threaded a needle and sewed a button on his coat, without taking the coat off—doing it as a man would do, contorting, pricking his fingers, making remarks while he concentrated on the task. With him, it was spontaneous and unrehearsed, the way it had once been done almost forgotten. But it pleased the audience. They rocked with laughter. They were with him again, clay for the moulding.

He was only well launched into the more serious part of his lecture when they heard it again—the same sort of sound which had shattered the calm of the previous evening. Whooping, yelling, shooting, cowboys, drawing gradually nearer, riding as before, at a dead run.

Gentleman Jim paused. The night before, most of the boys, at least, had been out to hooray the Professor, to have their fun. It had gone a bit far, but most of them had had no serious intent. Still, the leader had been paid, as he had admitted.

For the same thing to happen again tonight was different. It was not original, but neither would it be in fun. The quality of the yells denoted that. There was a savage cadence in the shouts tonight which had been absent the first time.

They were outside now, circling the tent, shooting at the sky. Faces lost their colour, but all were looking to the Professor. Then the horsemen came surging inside, again in a repeat performance.

But here too was a difference. One glance was enough to show Gentleman Jim that these men were not cowboys, though they knew how to ride well enough and were dressed in range regalia. Theirs were faces which the sun seldom had a chance to touch, pasty, shifty-eyed. Hard faces, such as would gather at no respectable ranch. These were hangers-on from the saloons, recruited and sent here by Deal Hathaway. They hadn't come for fun—not tonight—not any of them. Again the guns were blazing, not entirely at the ceiling of the tent. Gentleman Jim heard the eerie whine of a bullet just above his head as the horsemen surged toward him.

Then, pulling their mounts to a sliding stop, the foremost rider was shaking out a loop in a long cast—aimed for Jim's neck. 'I play rough—when I have to!'

67

## CHAPTER SEVEN

# IMPELLING REASONS

There was no horseplay here. This was in dead earnest, under the cloak of foolery. Gentleman Jim threw up his arm, moving fast. But the man in the saddle was no tenderfoot where a rope was concerned. He had built this loop wide, too big to dodge or throw off, and he was narrowing it with deadly speed and precision as it settled.

Gentleman Jim felt it closing, and he knew what the next move would be—the horse whirling, dragging him off his feet. If the rope closed around his throat, the jerk would break his neck as quickly as a drop from the tree in the coulee beyond. If it caught him lower down, the end result would be the same, only more painful and longer delayed.

And he was caught. Up to that point, a man had a chance to fight back, to try and save himself. Once the noose had closed, he was as helpless as a cayuse or cow against the rope. There was too much leverage on the other end, with a half-hitch around a saddle horn and a buck-jumping cayuse to take up the slack and keep it tight. Where a thousand pounds of fighting animal could only give in, a man could do even less.

He felt the rope tightening, knew that despite the burning sting of it along the edge of his hand that his thrust had failed. It was going to settle and close where the thrower had intended, around his neck.

Another man was lunging to his feet, directly in front of him. He had been on the front row of benches, crowded in among several others in this overflow crowd, so that Gentleman Jim had failed to notice him particularly. Now, as he lunged forward, he recognized him. This was the cowboy, Bill Bender, who had led the riders the evening before, the man he had jerked off his horse and made to get down on his knees.

Ironically enough, it was what Bender had done then that was making this attack so sure-fire tonight. Plenty of people had seen how the Professor had handled him then, and Bender was known to be salty. This other man, forewarned, was taking no chances, giving none to the word-shark.

But what neither of them had calculated on was Bender. There was no liquor in him tonight, no bribe in his pocket. Something different had brought him back to the lecture this time, and he was a fast-thinking, fast-moving man in a crisis. He was jerking a knife from a pocket even as he came lunging to his feet. The next instant the *razor* edge slashed through the tightening rope as a wolf's teeth would snap through flesh and bone incautiously exposed to its reach.

If the surprise attack with the noose had been too fast for Gentleman Jim, the unexpectedness of this was equally disconcerting to the man on horseback, and to those who rode with him. By this time, a score of men were on their feet and surging forward, outraged. They understood what was being attempted, and horseplay was one thing. Murder under its guise was quite another.

It was frightening how fast men could be transformed from sober citizens intent on mildly uplifting entertainment to a ravening pack athirst for blood. They were dragging the invaders from their saddles, and cries of 'Lynch him!' drowned out the tumult which had rocked the tent moments before. This was a righteous anger, and twice as deadly on that account.

Gentleman Jim threw off his hempen necktie, breathing heavily for a moment. Events were crowding themselves. But he had not received the name by which he was known solely because of an unruffled manner or the ability to wear his clothes well. There was a coolness underlying the manner, and it did not desert him now.

They were starting to hustle the rope thrower toward the entrance, and the wrath of the crowd was growing with each step taken. Nearly every man in the big tent was joining in the rush.

There was no doubt that the victim deserved what they intended that he should get. But the idea was revolting, and it was against the sort of progress and order that he was advocating from this town. Gentleman Jim moved fast.

He circled and reached the doorway ahead of them, and there was a quality in his voice which caught their attention above the savagery of their own shouts.

'Hold up a minute, friends! Let's do everything fairly and in order—that's what we're here for!'

They looked up at him, startled, hesitating, and he went on quickly.

'Don't think for a moment that I don't appreciate what you folks have in mind. My own basic feelings run right along with yours. But we don't progress when we fail to rise above our baser instincts, nor do we build a community to be proud of. And since it was me that he tried to rope and hog-tie, I think I've a right to a voice in the matter.'

'He was aimin' to break yore neck in cold blood, Professor,' one man protested. 'We saw it all—as dirty and cowardly a trick as was ever pulled. Hangin's too good for him!'

71

'Sure it is,' Gentleman Jim concurred readily. 'So it would be a shame to hang him, wouldn't it?'

They were taken aback by that retort.

'But what else is there to do? What's worse—'

'It might be a worse punishment for him to have to stay and listen to me talk,' Gentleman Jim suggested whimsically. 'In any case, we don't want his blood on our hands, and we do want to do things in a legal and civilized manner. Let's get the horses back outside—what I said last night still applies, I think—and these other men can sit up in front and listen.'

Passions, swiftly roused, were cooling under his half-humorous handling of the situation, and the idea appealed to those who had been so ready to lynch the mobsters. The men who had ridden in so brazenly were docile now, cowed by the rage which beat at them. Though there were dissenters among the crowd.

'You're a good hand at yore own game, Professor,' one man protested. 'But these hellions are about as unregenerate a bunch as could be rounded up this side of hell itself. I'm plumb doubtful that even you can do anything with 'em.'

It was Bill Bender, who had led the raid the evening before, then had jumped so quickly to slash the rope tonight and avert disaster, who took issue with that.

'Might be that you're barkin' at the wrong gopher hole, Boggs,' he protested. 'You know me well enough. I been pretty much of a hellion, I guess, always up to somethin', some of it just plain meanness, like when I come in here last night to hooray the Professor.'

'Yeah, you been plenty big for your breeches, Bill. Ain't no doubt about that.'

'That's what I mean. I kind of liked to make my brag that nobody'd curried me—nor ever would. That I was tough. But the way the Professor set me down last night, sure give me a jolt. Never had nothin' like that happen to me before. Well—' he looked around, half defiantly, half challengingly.

'If a man like him can do that, he's got all I ever had—and somethin' besides! So I'm here tonight to listen to him again! Sounds to me like he's talkin' common sense for all of us. What I was gettin' at is, that if it has that effect on me, it can sort of jar these other fellows, too!'

His words were making an impression on the crowd, many of whom were resuming their seats. But some were unconvinced.

'Sure you've been a hellion, Bill,' one of the business men who had attended the noon meeting spoke up. He had an undershot jaw like a bulldog, and stubbornness was in his voice. 'We all know that. But these others—they come in here to kill. They wouldn't do that of their own accord—and specially on horseback, fixed up like cowhands, which they ain't! Who sent you here?' he demanded.

Gentleman Jim placed a hand on his shoulder and pushed him back toward a seat.

'That's an interesting question, Mr. Staves,' he conceded. 'But this is not the moment for an inquisition. We are here for a purpose, and if we digress from it, we are the losers, and those who would create dissension among us are the gainers. An orderly community can come about only if there is first an orderly life among its individuals.'

He was talking again now, once more in control of the situation, with the crowd behind him. Briefly he found time to wonder at himself. What was he trying to do, anyway? Did he know himself?

*You're getting so wrapped up in being the Professor that you're forgetting who you are!* he thought sarcastically. *You're Gentleman Jim Thornton—a rather good-looking, gifted tramp who's progressed steadily on the downhill track from confidence man to the point where you associate with highwaymen and cold-blooded killers like the Weasel and Big Nose Sullivan! You're here for the purpose of robbing these*

74

*people!*

To these people, he was Timothy Meader, the Professor. A sort of an apostle of uplift. His job was to show them the way and fight for them to get what they wanted. But he was far from being a professor or an uplifter. He'd been talking about hellions as unregenerate as could be found this side of the grave. What else than that was he?

And yet—he'd gotten himself into this, and now he had to go ahead with it. Not only for practical reasons, but because he couldn't let them down. It was all mixed up, but that was the way it was.

It was over with, finally. Men and women congratulated him warmly, but the words had an empty sound. Though the trouble was with him, not them. He reached his room, Happy silent beside him, and sank down on the bed, staring at space.

'Happy,' he said, 'I was a fool to come here.'

Happy eyed him uncertainly, but offered no comment.

'I didn't realize what I was letting myself in for,' Gentleman Jim went on. 'Me, to lead a crusade! For that's what it amounts to. To clean up this town! That's the sheriff's job, isn't it? Me, Gentleman Jim Thornton!'

'It's hell,' Happy agreed unhappily. But still he had no suggestion, though advice usually flowed profusely from his tongue.

Had he but realized it, Happy was as bewildered in mind as Gentleman Jim himself. There had been fun and entertainment for a while tonight, as usual. But when Gentleman Jim had gotten well launched into his topic, responsibility both personal and civic, there had been a power to his words, a conviction which gripped the group. Nor had its effect been confined only to those down in the audience. Crouching there behind the organ, Happy had listened, as stirred as any of them. This was not the Gentleman Jim that he had known, nor the man play-acting as being a professor.

Given the choice of attending such a meeting, Happy would have shied away as violently as a once-bitten cayuse from the smell of rattlesnake. But he had to attend, and he had been caught completely off guard by this transformation. He had listened to a man who had something to say, and now he was baffled, upset, more completely unhappy than he had ever been before. And a morose view of life had earned him his nickname.

'Seems to me,' he said cautiously, 'that you're gettin' into a mess—because you kind of believe what you're tellin' them!'

Gentleman Jim looked at him.

'That's the hell of it,' he said. 'When I get up to talk, I'm just going to tell them what they want to hear. And then, first thing, I'm believing it myself! I've got to walk,' he added huskily. 'I can't sit still—nor go to bed. I've got to get out and walk!'

Happy understood that. Only when Gentleman Jim was profoundly disturbed or upset did he have to walk and straighten himself out. Some men took to drink at such a time, others to various diversions, but Gentleman Jim walked. Those times, with him, were rare. Usually he could give a decision in a split second, without turning a hair.

Knowing that he liked to be alone at such a time, Happy watched in fresh uncertainty.

'Keep yore eyes open, Jim,' he cautioned. 'Like it or not, you've sure let yoreself in for trouble, stirrin' up a plumb hornets' nest. Might be they won't try a rope, next time—but a bullet!'

Gentleman Jim eyed him strangely.

'That, at least, would resolve a lot of questions,' he said, and went out into the night.

But he had no intention of being a target if it could be avoided, and swung away from the main part of town, out into the lonely quiet of the country. His mind, weary with his other problem, left off gnawing at that one for a while to dwell on the easier one which Happy had tossed his way.

The man who had tried to rope him had

remained for the full programme, along with his companions. They had been scared, frightened of what the still angry crowd would do to them if they refused. What effect the lecture might have had on them, Gentleman Jim had no idea. Not much, he suspected. They were about as tough a crew as could be assembled, and with no interest in building up the town or in such things as responsibility. Those who came because they wanted to hear that sort of thing, liked it. No one else could be expected to.

Happy had had no delusions as to what the invaders had come for, or why. Neither, apparently, had the crowd, men like Boggs, who had been ready for direct action, more than willing to perpetuate the type of action which had given the town its name, the very thing that they were trying to get away from.

Well, he had challenged Deal Hathaway that day, and Hathaway had put it up to him to go along and share the gravy, or take the consequences. That was the basic issue—Hathaway or himself. The rest was all beside the point. And Hathaway had warned that when he played at all, he played rough.

No one but Hathaway could have gathered such a crew and gotten them to ride on such an errand. They had intended to mask it as horseplay, until the deed was done, and then, by moving fast, to be out of the way. They counted on Deal Hathaway to protect them, once they had done his job for him.

Which meant that they believed Hathaway could do it. There was the law—as represented by Paul Hoffman. But the sheriff was an uncertain quantity. Or perhaps Hathaway knew where he stood.

It all added up to the certainty of more trouble. Wearily, Gentleman Jim brushed that aside as unimportant. He knew how to meet such a danger, and it did not worry him unduly. This other matter, however, troubled him as nothing had ever done before.

*I should be with him—not fighting him,* he thought. *What's come over me? Whatever I do, I'm fighting myself, too!*

When he finally returned, physically tired, and crawled into bed beside the peacefully sleeping Happy, there was still no answer, no peace for him.

'I could ride out and not come back,' he thought, staring at the darkness. And shook his head. That would be no answer. Besides, there were reasons, impelling ones, why he was through with running. One of them was a girl, asleep in another room of this same house. The paramount reason, all in one. The half-truth was in his mind, that he was doing this against all that he had ever been or done, to please her. Even though such a course must lead inevitably to disaster.

## CHAPTER EIGHT

# INTERRUPTION

There was a brooding quietness over Hangman's Coulee today which was like a July afternoon with thunderheads building up at the edge of the hills. The rumbling echoes of that storm sounded as Gilson returned home for the midday meal.

'Some of the committee had a talk with Hathaway this morning,' he announced. 'They accused him of setting Ten-Spot Lolo and his crew on you last night, Professor.'

Maita looked up quickly, the colour draining from her cheeks. Gentleman Jim, buttering a slice of bread, paused. Outwardly he was as cool as ever.

'Weren't the committee a little hasty?' he asked.

'Hathaway didn't admit it, of course—but he didn't deny it,' Gilson retorted. 'There's no question but what he was responsible. Ten-Spot is keeping out of sight today, and so are the rest of that bunch. But Hathaway did say that we'd asked for trouble, and could have as much as we wanted.'

80

'Showdown, eh?'

'That's what it amounts to. He said that he'd pledged five thousand dollars toward the railroad, and he intended to pay as he promised, because he thought the railroad would be a good thing. But that he had no use for hymn-singers or uplifters, and he'd fight us to the last ditch on that proposition. So now we know where we stand.'

Gentleman Jim lifted a hand to twist his moustache, and checked the motion, remembering that the moustache was gone. But this was one more reason why he couldn't run out now. He had been merely the instrument for a policy, but he had brought this about, and in a way he admired Deal Hathaway. Had he come here in his right guise, instead of as an exponent of civic betterment, he and Hathaway would have been friends.

Hathaway was what he was, and determined to pursue his own course, no matter what the cost. It took courage to make such a stand, particularly against many of the men who had been, nominally, at least, his friends.

But that seemed a minor problem compared to his own. He had made no direct move toward the goal which had brought him here in the first place, the matter of getting his hands on that hundred thousand dollars of railroad money. More money than he had ever tried to get at one time before. But that was just one of his troubles.

The money was not yet all collected, so there was no rush where it was concerned. The thing which puzzled and almost frightened him was what he would do when the time came, how far he would pursue this course on which he had embarked. When he got up as the Professor, he seemed to be a different man.

The town was taking on a holiday aspect, with a look something like that of an old-time camp meeting, such as he dimly remembered from when he was a small boy. People living far out in the country were coming in, driving with lumber wagons loaded with provisions, cooking utensils, tents and blankets. A dozen smaller tents were already pitched near the big one, back beside the creek which curved as if to avoid the contaminations of that grim tree which had given the town its name.

More tents would be pitched before night. Word had spread, and it had been favourable. The Professor wasn't trying to sell them anything. He was entertaining and instructive, as promised, and there was the expectation of something bigger—something dramatic—that everyone could sense.

There would be bigger crowds for every meeting. So, to accommodate the increasing numbers, a dozen volunteers had been at work today. The log benches had been extended on either side, leaving a narrower aisle. This would preclude any possibility of horses being ridden inside the tent again, though there was scant likelihood of another such performance being attempted.

Up front, a board platform had been built, raised nearly three feet off the ground, twenty feet wide. The speaker's stand was now up on that, as was the organ. That would be better, and by moving it back as far as possible, it also gave more room down in front.

'By the time you've been here three weeks, this will be a different community, just as we've hoped for,' Maita commented. 'All that most people require is to be set to thinking, giving some leadership. They're tired of the way things have been run.' She hesitated, added shyly, 'I had heard that you were rather wonderful at this work, but the results that you've gotten already are extraordinary.'

Three weeks! He had planned to get out, after a week at most. This was just one more hazard which he had failed to foresee, Gentleman Jim realized. For he didn't like the idea of going on—back to an old life suddenly blank and without promise.

Yet what else could he do? Unwittingly, he was tying himself hand and foot. If he

83

remained, anything that he did would be wrong. This was Deal Hathaway's town. Big Nose Sullivan and the Weasel would be coming along, depending on him to make good. While in the background was the law—

'Hoist by his own petard,' he muttered. 'Now I know what that means. I've had a taste of respectability, and I like it—and it's as far out of reach as the moon!'

Happy was getting the hang of his job. For the first couple of evenings he had been nervous, fearful in his playing of unaccustomed songs, of assisting with the lantern slides. Now, as he confessed, he sort of liked it. The organ music rolled out, and Gentleman Jim observed that Ten-Spot Lolo was in the crowd again. This time he was off at the side, as unobtrusive as possible. But he was there, in a fresh shirt and with slicked-back hair. There was no sign of any of his companions.

'There are just two kinds of people,' Gentleman Jim said, once he had launched into his talk. 'The kind who follow— generally blindly, allowing others to lead them, being shaped by their environment, by whatever forces surround them. And the kind who shape the forces and their own lives, who emerge as leaders.

'When you look at them, there may not be much outward difference. Two arms, two legs, two eyes, two ears, one nose, hair on the top of the head. They walk the same and talk the same language. But the one man is a slave, and the other man is free. One man pursues his destiny, the other is pursued by it until overtaken and bound in chains which he has unwittingly helped to contrive.'

*Here I go again*, he thought, surprised. Somehow, when he got up here, he seemed to be a new man, outside himself.

'This community is a good example of what I mean,' he went on, more deliberately now. 'We have examples of both types. Those who are not satisfied with an environment which tends to make slaves of all whom it encompasses, which lowers men to a standard little above that of beasts. But there are those who like that sort of thing, and others who work for it because they are hired to do so. Which is a sure way to bind fetters upon your own feet.

'You've all tried to walk in mud. It's not easy, is it? The farther you go, the more mud clings to your feet, weighing you down until soon it is almost impossible to go at all. That's the way slavery grows unless we get away from it, out of the mud. In fact—'

There was a commotion near the rear of the tent. Someone had stood up abruptly, shouting words which sounded like *Liar* and *Scoundrel*. Gentleman Jim couldn't quite catch it, because several of those back there had jumped up just as promptly and were hustling the objector outside, not too gently. They were that strange mixture which is human—avid to hear what the Professor had to say, ready to agree with him on all general principles, yet swift to take offence at an interruption and to deal roughly with any offender. There had been too many disturbances at these meetings, and their mood was touchy.

'Now stay out!' The words came back, faintly, then the self-appointed vigilance committee were quietly re-entering, taking their seats again. A ripple ran around the tent, subsided. Gentleman Jim went on without comment. But it was more than ever as if another man than himself was doing the talking. There had been something in that half-glimpse of the other man, some quality in that voice shouting *Liar*, which had stirred memory in him. As though a ghost had entered the tent.

Memory was an elusive thing. It hovered at the fringes of his consciousness, and would come no nearer. A wild notion did come to him for a moment, but he dismissed it, since reason assured him that it was impossible.

Probably that had been someone sent over here by Deal Hathaway to heckle him. It would be like the gambler to create a minor disturbance until he was ready for some big stroke again.

The worst of it was that the fellow, whoever he was, had been right. *Liar!* What else was he than that, standing up here, talking about something that he had never believed in? Pretending to be a leader, a civic-minded man, when he consorted with killers, when he was here to rob these who were supporting him! *Scoundrel!* There were no more apt words in the language than those which had been hurled at him.

Something bigger than himself was here, and was he controlling it, or it him? And which way did he want it?

But this speaker was not himself, any more than he was Timothy Meader just because he stood here in the garments of the Professor. This stranger was still talking, as impellingly as he had done the night before.

The prick of his own mind, the contempt which he felt for himself even as he uttered the words, seemed like the spur to a cayuse. Much as he might hate the goad, it drove him on to do his best.

Maita Gilson, seated near the front, was watching him with shining eyes. He took his own away from her with an effort, and stared at sight of Deal Hathaway, near the opposite side of the tent from Ten-Spot Lolo.

One look at the saloon-keeper was enough to show that he, at least, had not fallen under the spell of this lecture. He had come to listen and see for himself, but he was not impressed. His lips curled back scornfully, as he met Gentleman Jim's look. Then, deliberately, he stood up, lifted the flap at the side and went out into the night.

Few had noticed him. But there was contempt and assurance in the man. Qualities which did not have the power to disturb Gentleman Jim. But something else did have the ability. He was talking himself into a corner—into a position from which soon there would be no retreat.

'Ye're a scoundrel and a liar, I say, and tonight ye die for the black-hearted ingrate and hypocrite that ye are!'

It was the same voice that had created the earlier disturbance. He couldn't mistake it—not ever again. And now the face was before him as well—a face lined and weather-beaten, showing the marks of the years, of time which had not dealt gently. It was capped by thinning white hair, the eyes fanatical and gleaming.

No retreat! And here was something which he certainly had not counted on—further fruits of the part he was playing, of a benevolent professor while plotting robbery!

The old man had raised up suddenly,

crawling out from under the platform on which Gentleman Jim stood. After being thrown out, he must have crept back under the edge of the tent and so in under the shelter of the newly raised platform.

Now, as he made his denunciation and raised to his trembling erectness, a thin shabby figure, he held a six-gun. In the sudden silence the click of the hammer was loud and unmistakable as he eared it back.

## CHAPTER NINE

## HAPPY'S CONFESSION

Here was fanaticism, but it was more than that. This was hatred, dark as the brooding shadows of the tree in the coulee behind them. On other occasions, when peril threatened, Gentleman Jim had been swift to respond, but now he seemed frozen.

But the old man was slow, and his purpose motivated him to the exclusion of all else. He was too intent upon what he purposed doing to think about the crowd, but again they were upon him before he could shoot. Only his age and manifest frailness saved him from being hustled toward the hanging tree, for at this second threat to the professor their mood was angry.

They hustled him outside, sending him off with threats and imprecations. Threats to have him locked up, or to kill him if he interfered again. And while this went on just outside the tent, Gentleman Jim stood taut, his eyes still fixed on the spot where the old man had risen up so suddenly.

Liar! Black-hearted ingrate! The words had stabbed before, but they had been like thorns along the trail, ripping away a man's coat and shirt, scratching to the skin. This time, with protection torn off, they struck deep. He came quietly down from the platform, and now the excited audience was beginning to leave, the spell was broken. So quickly could one act undo a slow building up. Still, this opposition had only increased his popularity, fused the crowd behind him.

All that he wanted now was to get away, and there was no place to run. A man might walk half the night, deep into the desert, or climb the highest mountain, but he could not outrun his thoughts—or his conscience. What was it that Happy had said? That he had no conscience?

Not all of the crowd was leaving. Many were gathering around him, voicing their sympathy at the interruption and the threat to his life.

'We'll take steps to see that it don't happen again,' Staves declared. 'The old man is pretty much of a crackpot, I guess, but up to now he's at least been harmless enough. I think the best thing to do is to have the sheriff lock him up, where he can't cause any mischief.'

'No, don't do that,' Gentleman Jim protested. 'Let him alone. After all, he has a right to his own opinion.'

'But not to try and kill you because he disagrees,' Staves said stubbornly. 'If he was locked up, just while you're in the community—'

'No,' Gentleman Jim repeated. 'Let him alone.'

Others among them had a different proposal, which they broached now.

'There's a lot of folks have come in and are stayin' here, just to get the most out of these lectures and entertainment features you're givin',' it was explained. 'And most of them would sure enjoy listenin' to you twice a day, afternoons as well as evenin', if it wouldn't be too hard on you. Like Ma was sayin', it both rests a body and gives you somethin' worth while to think about, just listenin' to you.'

'Of course, if that's the way you want it, it can be arranged,' Gentleman Jim agreed abstractedly.

'Shall we say, starting tomorrow afternoon, then?'

'Why not?' he agreed.

Since that was customary, and what they wanted, it was the thing to do. A few hours earlier he would have been appalled. Now he was only listless. He had gotten himself into this, and it was like a rope around his neck, closing. A noose which he saw no way to throw off, which no one could slash for him. But his mind was far removed even from that aspect as he turned back toward the house.

Tonight, quite naturally, Maita walked beside him. She did not speak, nor seem to expect anything of him, respecting his mood. This quality of hers, of understanding and leaving a man to his own thoughts, was rare. But having her beside him was somehow comforting. Only when they paused outside the house did she speak.

'Something is troubling you,' she said, and half lifted her hand as if to lay it on his arm, then withdrew it. 'I wish that there was some way in which we could help. You're doing so much for us.'

As he made no reply, she went on, half timidly.

'It has to do with that man, doesn't it?—McGilroy is his name, I think. He lives a couple of miles out of town, just he and his wife. They're very poor. And, of course, they feel alien here, or I suppose they do, for they've always lived off by themselves and have been left pretty much alone—'

'He and his wife?' Gentleman Jim repeated. 'And they are poor, you say?'

'Very poor. And very much alone. He—well, they both seem a little strange; queer, perhaps, to the rest of us. Probably we seem as much so to them. What I mean is—I wouldn't take it too hard, the wild things he said about you—'

'It's usually the truth that hurts,' Gentleman Jim answered quietly. 'And I find that there's too much of truth in his words to brush them aside. But, thank you, Miss Maita. Your sympathy is a real comfort.'

He went on into his room, where he found Happy anxious to talk. Happy was in a state of jitters, and he had to talk—either that or go out and get drunk. Recognizing his condition, Gentleman Jim resigned himself to the inevitable.

'Now it's two meetings a day,' Happy complained. 'Think you can keep talkin' so much?'

'Words come easy,' Gentleman Jim sighed. 'I guess that's my trouble, Happy—they always have come easy.'

'So have a lot of other things,' Happy said shrewdly. 'But it looks to me like you're gettin' in over your depth, Jim. And makin' plenty of enemies. Keep on, and at one of these meetin's they'll be sayin' things over

93

you, droppin' clods on you with a few flowers to finish it off. That old geezer sure seems to have it in for you—and he ain't the only one.'

'You were wiser than I was, Happy,' Gentleman Jim confessed soberly, sinking down on the edge of the bed. 'You wanted to keep out of this, but I was so sure I could do it. And now—'

'Now the devil of it is that you *are* doing it,' Happy growled. 'I knew you could play any part you ever tried, Jim, even to actin' and talkin' like a professor. It was this uplift stuff that I was worried about. But the way you've been handlin' that—why, hell's bells, I bet you could give spades to a sky pilot when it comes to preachin' a sermon. You sound like you meant every word of it, while you're spoutin'.'

'I do, Happy. While I'm giving it.'

Happy stirred uneasily.

'You've got me goin',' he confessed. 'I—I almost fall for your line myself. And when *I* get to doing that, and you do it yourself—looks to me like we're really runnin' full tilt into trouble that'll make what we was in, when that posse was around the canyon, look like a picnic.'

## CHAPTER TEN

# A MATTER OF TRUST

Deal Hathaway had had a double purpose in attending the meeting, and the second part of it worked out better than he had hoped for. He had come, partly in the expectation that someone might heckle. From outside, he had seen the old man hustled way, following his second interruption. Here were dividends.

Hathaway was too shrewd a man to go to McGilroy with sympathy or offer of help. But he had plenty of men who could offer both without exciting suspicion, and some of these, presently, led the old man to Hathaway's saloon and so to his office.

That was not difficult, since McGilroy walked like a man in a daze. He had been hurt when thrown out, and blood was on his face, but he seemed unaware of that, muttering to himself. Only when he looked up and recognized Hathaway did the light of reason come into his eyes again. Then he glanced around the office, nervously.

'How—how'd I get here?' he demanded. 'Let me out of here!'

'Take it easy, old-timer,' Hathaway said soothingly. 'You're among friends. Here, have a drink.'

McGilroy pushed the bottle back angrily. 'No,' he refused. 'I don't want none of it!'

'But you hate this Professor, don't you?' Hathaway said. 'You've made that plain. Maybe we can work together. I don't like him any better than you do.'

McGilroy eyed him cunningly for a moment, then resentment came back to his eyes.

'I kill my own snakes,' he said. 'Let me out of here.'

'But be reasonable, man,' Hathaway protested. 'When we're both on the same side of the fence—'

'We ain't,' McGilroy grunted. 'And never could be.'

He got up and walked to the door. The others looked at Hathaway, but after a moment he shrugged his shoulders.

'Reckon I've been mistaken, too,' he said. 'Maybe this Professor is more of a guy than I figured him to be!'

★      ★      ★

Sam Staves had invited the Professor and the organist for dinner at his house today, and Gentleman Jim had accepted with some reluctance. Ordinarily he would have been pleased, for the dinner was sure to be sumptuous, their host gracious. The only

96

trouble was that today he would have preferred to be alone, off by himself. Which, as the Professor, was almost out of the question.

Arriving, they found that there were several other guests as well, including the banker and other carefully selected members of the original finance committee, whom he had met before. There was also Minerva Staves, Sam's sister, who had cooked the dinner. And who, taking pity on Happy's dolorous expression, set out to try and make him feel at home.

Like Happy, Minerva was past her first bloom, but like him, she too was an artist, in her way. Where he could coax melody from the battered keys of an old organ, drawing out its soul as few players knew how to do, Minerva was at her best on the culinary side. Today she had outdone herself with fluffy potatoes, rich brown gravy, fried chicken, dumplings and all the rest.

Watching her, Gentleman Jim thought that he understood some of her pleasure. Minerva Staves undoubtedly had a good home here with her stubborn, domineering brother. But she was completely under his subjection, and even company was probably a rare thing. Not all the colour in her cheeks came from bending over a hot stove. A part of it was the flush of excitement.

'Seems like since you and the Professor came to town, it's been a new place,' she confided to Happy. 'Folks are getting a new outlook on life—a new spirit. My, you'd ought to be happy.'

'I am,' Happy grunted. 'Only I don't feel thata way.'

At the other end of the table, Sam Staves was speaking in his usual forthright way.

'Reckon you've noticed, Professor, that there's just a few of the best of us here today, eh?' he said, with an attempt at lightness. 'What I mean is, from the committee that's collected the money for the railroad. This dinner ain't all for pleasure—though eatin' a good meal always gives me a lot of enjoyment. But it's partly business. We wanted to ask your advice—and mebby get your help.'

John Gilson nodded.

'That's so, Mr. Meader,' he agreed.

'What we're up against is a tougher situation than we had counted on, to start with,' Staves went on. 'Deal Hathaway, he was with us for a while—or we figured he was. Now he ain't making no bones about it that he's against you and most of the things we want to do in this town—and he's showin' it plain enough!' He looked at Gilson, who took up the thread.

'Deal Hathaway has been pretty much like any of the rest of us, outwardly, up to

98

now,' he said, choosing his words carefully. 'What I mean is, this is a new town—a raw town in many respects. There has been no church, no school, and few refining or softening influences. Under those conditions, all men who took anything like a prominent part or tried to get ahead, appeared pretty much alike. The differences didn't show too much. But now there is a dividing line.'

'I'll say there is!' Staves resumed. 'Hathaway claims that your lectures are getting folks in the mood for gettin' a preacher in here after you leave, and while we hadn't thought about that, I will say it might be a good idea. Anyway, he's takin' the bit in his mouth and stampedin' off the other way to make it more'n ever his sort of town. Know what he's done, only today?'

He looked around the table, breathing heavily, and wagged a finger at them.

'What he's done was to bring in two big wagon-loads of gamblin' tables this mornin', and now he's settin' them up in his saloon! Faro, roulette, everything like that. Now, we ain't been against that sort of thing, you understand. A man could have a game of poker, say, any time he felt like it. But we ain't been too strong for it, neither. Hathaway's bringin' in them things right now, looks to me like flauntin' it in our faces, that he's aimin' to run this town his way!'

Gentleman Jim helped himself to a fresh drumstick.

'A gesture of defiance, in other words?'

'Sure. And plenty of the boys of the town are int'rested, and flockin' there to try out his games. It's more'n a gesture. It's a counter-attraction, and a threat.'

Gentleman Jim did not feel like smiling, even to himself. On any other occasion he would have done so at the thought of being classed as a counter-attraction to a gambling game.

'But he ain't going to get away with it!' Staves exploded. 'We don't aim to take it layin' down.'

'That is the situation, outwardly,' John Gilson went on with his usual preciseness. 'Actually, what we are afraid of is something far worse. I'm not referring to McGilroy; for with him I imagine it's some fancied wrong and a personal affair. But there was that other attempt on your life the other night, Professor. I am pretty well convinced that Deal Hathaway was behind that, and while, of course, he hasn't admitted it, neither has he denied it. If he will go that far, there is no limit to what he may try.'

'Go ahead and tell him, Johnny,' Staves urged. 'You know how to do it.'

'We are all agreed upon what I have to say,' Gilson conceded. 'Even so, I hesitate

100

to voice such sentiments about any man. Only the urgency of the situation compels us to do so. As a matter of fact, there have been several unexplained happenings in this town in the not too recent past which now have taken on new significance. Robberies, killings—aside from the hangings which have been a blot upon our community—all more or less customary occurrences in such a town as this. But the ugly thing is that we think we begin to see a pattern.'

'What we're wonderin' is, if Deal Hathaway won't boggle at tryin' to get rid of you, even by murder, and is settin' himself up as boss of the bad men, if he ain't been headin' them up all along,' Staves said bluntly. 'And I don't care how soon he hears that I've said it!'

The others looked grave. This was bringing hidden fears and suspicions out into the open, and there were bound to be repercussions. Here too, Gentleman Jim knew, was the real issue, of which his coming had been only a cloak and a diversion. Again Gilson took up the thread of the narrative.

'To come to the point, Professor, what we are wondering about is this: A hundred thousand dollars is a lot of money—a sum to make the hauls of most robberies, even those committed well to the south of us by Big Nose Sullivan's gang, seem picayune. It has occurred to us that maybe Deal Hathaway has contributed toward that hundred thousand, as a gesture and a bait. But that, with it collected, he would have more interest in having his gang steal it than in turning it over to the railroad!'

'Mebby we're doing him an injustice,' Boggs commented quietly. 'I sure hope we are. We are telling you this, Professor, knowing that we can trust you. You've showed yoreself to be just the sort we hoped you would be, to help us get public opinion kind of on the right track, so we could work out to do something here. Now we want your advice and help. What we have thought—and talked about, in this room, won't go any farther. But if we're right, then we'd be mighty foolish not to take precautions.'

'Exactly,' Gilson agreed. 'I am not exaggerating in saying that some of Deal Hathaway's preparations in the past few days have alarmed us. And it is well known that he controls a number of men, in one way or another. Which adds up to a risk, particularly since we have the full sum guaranteed to the railroad collected now. As he is, of course, aware. There has been another hitch—perhaps contrived—and the representatives from the railroad won't be along to pick it up for at least several days. So we are concerned with keeping it safe until we can turn it over to them.'

Gentleman Jim eyed them in amazement.

'I can understand that. But isn't the logical move to put it in your bank, John?'

Ruefully, Gilson shook his head.

'It isn't generally known,' he explained. 'But our bank was robbed about a month ago. This is known, of course. What folks don't know is that the robbers wrecked our safe, though they didn't find much in it. I have ordered a new safe, but it hasn't arrived. The wagon carrying the first one to be shipped, went off a cliff and everything was wrecked. It looked like an accident—but I have my doubts, particularly since some of these other things have happened. Another safe has been ordered and is on the way, but it will be some days before it can arrive.

'What I'm getting at is this: That for the present there is no safety in putting that money in the bank. And Deal Hathaway knows that as well as any of us. So we are concerned with some plan—some ruse, perhaps—which will ensure keeping it secure.'

For the first time, Gentleman Jim had difficulty in keeping a straight face.

'Why not sent it out of town?' he suggested.

'We've thought of that. But if we try it, the odds are heavy that a robbery will be attempted. If any one of this group goes—they'll guess pretty well what he carries with him. If we go outside this group—well, the plain fact is that we don't know who to trust, beyond the few of us who are here!'

*Here's where the devil must be laughing!* Gentleman Jim thought, but there was no amusement for him in the reflection. For these men to consult him on such a matter was cause for sardonic mirth, but they were speaking to him as Professor Timothy Meader. But Gilson's next words really startled him.

'What we have in mind, Professor, is this: That we might entrust the money to you for keeping. The last place where anyone would suspect it of being would be in the possession of a man of your vocation.'

## CHAPTER ELEVEN

## A BOLD BLUFF

Happy had been eating and talking, with more animation than he often showed, to Minerva Staves. Now he seemed to choke on his food, until his face grew red. But no one else had much time for that. Gentleman Jim's face, thanks to his training, betrayed nothing of his thoughts.

He should, he knew, have been filled with elation. He had come here to find some way to get hold of that money, and not in his wildest dreams had he expected that they would offer it to him, urge him to take it. Here was success, without the lifting of a hand.

But something had happened to him since he had arrived in this town. Exactly what it was, he did not know. Probably it was a combination of events, such as the old man standing up and calling him a liar, and this girl who sat next to him now, and the fact that these men trusted him.

He was not even sure but that, when he went away from here, he would still take that money with him. Nor was he sure that he *would* take it. He did know that he was somehow shocked by the thing which had been suggested, that he did not want that money. His voice, as was usual in moments of stress, seemed almost to belong to another man, to come from his lips with cool detachment.

'That is an intriguing notion,' he confessed. 'The thought of an itinerant professor having a fortune in his keeping! I'm afraid the mere notion would bring heart-failure to me, if I were to take it seriously.'

'But we mean it seriously,' Staves

105

persisted. 'Ain't it a good idea? Even if you was suspected, you're not only an honest man, but a mighty good fighting man as well. The money'd be safe with you, if anywhere!'

'It's not that we want to get you into any more peril than you already are,' John Gilson added. 'Certainly we wouldn't consider that for a moment. But we don't think that anybody would even suspect you of being the custodian.'

Gentleman Jim hesitated, strongly tempted for a moment. Again he met Maita Gilson's eyes, steady and cool on his face, and felt his own go hot. He shook his head violently.

'Your plan has merit, there's no doubt of that,' he agreed. 'But I think perhaps I have a better notion. Why not turn the money over to Deal Hathaway to keep for you? Do it publicly, going there as a committee, and ask him to put it in his safe? He undoubtedly has one. That will guarantee it. His hands will be tied—providing he has any notions to the contrary.'

They eyed him for a moment in admiration tinged with amazement. Staves was laughing boisterously, and John Gilson reached across and grasped his hand.

'Professor,' he declared, 'you're not only a grand lecturer on the platform, you're a genius off it as well! The solution was so simple that we couldn't see it, but you did. We'll take the money over to Mr. Hathaway at once.'

## CHAPTER TWELVE

## MEMORIES

Back in their room for a few minutes, putting the finishing touches to his appearance before the afternoon entertainment, Gentleman Jim waited for an outburst from Happy. But that gentleman was strangely silent, a far-away look in his eyes. Impatiently, Gentleman Jim broke the silence.

'Well, why don't you go ahead and tell me how many kinds of a fool I am?' he demanded.

Happy looked at him and shook his head.

'You mean, about that money?' he asked. 'I never was fretted up about it in the first place. It was you that wanted it—and the Weasel and Big Nose. And I sure don't figure we owe them anything. If you don't want it now—well, I don't blame you, Jim. This is a—a hell of a situation.' He grinned sheepishly at himself in the glass as he slicked down his hair.

'Gosh, look at me! You got me to the

point, with all this talk of buildin' a better community by havin' better folks in it, where I'm watchin' myself so that I'm almost afraid to use a cuss word! I never thought I'd come to that. But there ain't no other word for it. It is a hell of a situation.'

'You're right, there.'

'Yeah. But did you taste them biscuits that Minerva made? Talk about meltin' in your mouth! I never knew what that meant, before, except mebby with snow, but I do now! And fried chicken! All I ever used to think there was to a chicken was the head and tail pieces. And she's one woman that you can talk to real friendly and sensible!'

'You too, Happy?' Gentleman Jim eyed him with commiseration. 'How old are you, Happy?'

'Who? Me? How old? Why, le'see; I'm about forty-seven, near as I recall. Born the winter of the big snow, I was always told, and they used to say that was in—Eh? What's how old I am got to do with it? I look older'n what I am, I guess. Why?'

'But you're not too old to fall in love either, eh? Yes, it's a bad situation, all right.'

Happy stared blankly.

'Love?' he repeated. 'Now what you blatherin' about? You ain't meanin'— Minerva and me?' Colour washed up from his scrawny neck to burn across his face.

'Why—you gone plumb crazy, Jim?'

'I guess so,' Gentleman Jim admitted wryly. 'I must have. I've fallen in love with Maita Gilson—there's no use in boggling at the truth, for it's happened. And it looks as if you've fallen for Minerva—or at least for her cooking.'

'Hell's bells,' Happy swore helplessly, and collapsed on the edge of the bed, staring at his big companion with blank dismay. 'In love,' he repeated, and shuddered violently. 'I—maybe you're right. I don't care a—a blast about her cooking,' he said vigorously. 'Oh, I mean it's fine, but it's Minerva I like—she treats me like I was a human being. About the only person that ever did, except you. But—oh, hell and wild horses, Jim. If you're right about this—'

'We're a pair of prize fools, eh?'

Happy still looked dazed.

'Fools don't half say it,' he gulped. 'In love! And that sheriff hangin' around like a hound sniffin' for a fresh trail! Love! Mebby you know more about it than I do. There ain't nothin' like this ever happened to me before—'

'Nor to me,' Gentleman Jim said sharply. 'But I'm just beginning to face up to the facts, or some of them, for the first time in my life. And I don't like them. I'm sorry about you, Happy. I got you into this.'

'I tagged along,' Happy grunted. 'And

109

you got me out of more'n one mean fix.' He stood up and shook his head. 'Well, we better be gettin' over to the tent. You're in this worse than I am, Jim. And you always been able to find a way out of any fix we ever got in yet.' The trace of a rare grin lightened his face for a moment.

'In love,' he repeated. 'Well, I guess it is a—a mess, but I dunno but what I kind of enjoy it, at that.'

Gentleman Jim eyed him sharply, and hid a grin. No wonder that Happy wasn't worrying about that money. If only he had Happy's faith in his own ability to find a way out. So far as he could see, there was only darkness and trouble ahead, with no light anywhere.

He raised his head, staring unseeingly out of the window. Up to now, so engrossed had he been in other matters, he had not even thought about what he was going to speak on this afternoon. Now a slow look of concentration, almost of peace, settled on his face.

★     ★     ★

The audience was tent-filling again this afternoon. It was a warm day, sultry under the canvas. The edges had been raised and tied back on every side, to allow such breeze as there was to temper the heat, and one could look out, to the town on one side, to the cool stream and the Tree on the other. Cattle grazed in the distance, a lone horseman jogged down the winding road which led to the town.

It was a scene of peace. Outwardly there was nothing to indicate strife in this town, or in the hearts of men. As the notes of the last song died away, Gentleman Jim stepped forward.

'Friends,' he said quietly, 'I'm going to just give you a talk this afternoon—a story, you might say, instead of a lecture. It has been brought home to me that one of the foundations for a better community, of which I have been talking, is honesty—and that begins with the individual. So I'm going to be honest with you folks—and with myself. I hope you'll bear with me.'

Every eye was on him, interested, expectant.

'I suppose that most of you have had experiences similar, in some respects at least, to my own,' he added, while Happy watched in sudden anxiety. 'But I am thinking of something which happened a number of years ago. Many of the years between have been turbulent ones, but what I look back on contain memories both pleasant and bitter.'

This was a new mood upon him today, and Happy was quick to sense it. But how

111

much, and what, did he intend to tell? That was one thing about Gentleman Jim Thornton—he was unpredictable in his way of doing things.

'Some are pleasant memories, for numbered among them are the happiest of my boyhood, and surely there is no time in all of life which is so rich, or at least should be, as childhood. My own boyhood was turbulent. I was orphaned at the age of six. We were travelling in a covered wagon, my father and mother and I. A lone wagon on a lonely road—and Indians attacked it. I saw my parents killed. But, somehow, in the wreck of the overturned wagon, deep under the pile of canvas, the Indians overlooked me, not knowing that there was a third possible victim. The next day, still crouching there, shivering in terror, I was found by one of the finest men I have ever known, and his equally fine wife.'

His voice had grown husky, but it did not falter.

'They were driving along that same trail, fortunately now free of Indians, and they rescued me and took me in. They saved my life. They had few earthly possessions, but what they had they shared with me. They buried my parents. Then they took their places with me as well as love could teach them how. My foster-father was a great gentleman. His wife, my foster-mother, was a great lady.

'Not that they had wealth, or social position or great learning. Nothing like that. Those are outward signs by which some of us are prone to judge, forgetting that it is the heart which counts.'

Happy was watching him, startled. This was a new side of Gentleman Jim, a chapter of his history which he had never heard before, nor guessed at.

'They took me to the home which they had made, and treated me as their own son,' Gentleman Jim went on. 'No boy could ask for a finer father or mother. They did their best to teach me the simple fundamentals by which men live—faith and hope and charity. Honesty and courage and patience. I am afraid they failed. Not because of any lack of their own efforts or kindness, but because of my own perverseness.'

He was staring off into space as he spoke, not down at the intent faces of the audience. It was as though he looked into the past.

'Some devil seemed to have entered into me, when I saw my own parents butchered. There was iron in my soul, and at times it came to the fore. Oh, I had my good moments, I expect. I did learn to love my foster-parents, to appreciate what they had done for me. Never doubt it. Many a night, as I grew older, and went to the town three miles away, and remained there later than I was supposed to—later than they liked—I was ashamed of myself. But I stayed. Still, no matter how late the hour, when I finally stumbled home—sometimes with halting steps because of drink—there was always a light in the window, set there to guide and to welcome me back.'

This time he was silent for a full minute, and his voice had grown grim. No one stirred.

'I must have been a sore trial to them. But they did their best, and they never stopped loving me. They had lost their own son, not long before my own parents were killed. He had been about the age that I was when they found me. I turned out to be a very poor, a most disappointing substitute; I know that now. But still they loved me.

'As I say, I was perverse. It was as though there was a devil in me, making me do the things which, in my better moments, I hated. While the things that I really wanted to do seemed ever to go undone. The result—'

Again he paused, and now his tone was tight.

'A small circus came to town. My foster-parents regarded the circus as of the devil. Their own upbringing had been very strict. But I went anyway. I got drunk. Then I went home and stole the small accumulation of savings which my folks kept. I knew where it was. I knew—God help me—that my dear mother saw me take it. She did not say anything, nor try to stop me. But the look on her face, as I turned and saw her, the pain in it—it haunts me yet!

'Fool that I was, I ran back to the town. I went away with the circus. The memory of that look on her face, the knowledge of how deeply I had hurt her—I think it made me worse, not better. I never returned. Once I intended to, hoping to beg their forgiveness, in some small way to try and make restitution. But I found out then, too late, that they had gone away years before. Where, no one knew, but report had it that they were dead.'

Again he was silent, and something like a sigh ran through the assembled audience. This Professor knew about life and its problems, when he spoke. They could see the tense lines in his face, the look deep in his eyes.

'That isn't all the story,' he added, more quietly. 'It comes down to the present. To something that impels me to tell you this. Last night, in the rear of this tent, a man stood up and shouted that I was a liar. He was hustled out, and rather roughly treated. It seemed to me that I had heard a ghost, or seen one. It was as though that had been the accusing voice of my foster-father. Yet I had been told that they were both dead, and so forever beyond my reach, to ask their forgiveness.

'It was like the voice of conscience. I was troubled, but confused. Then, near the close of the meeting, it happened again. The same man. Calling me liar and scoundrel. Intending to shoot me—as I so richly deserved. For what else was I than liar and scoundrel, and worse? Thief and robber and black-hearted hypocrite. I did not blame him. But still I could not bring myself to believe.'

He looked around, and his voice was more gentle now.

'It seemed too good to believe—that Providence would grant me another chance. And the years had made many changes, ravaging that face. But I have learned since that this man who so rightly accused me was named McGilroy. That he lives, with his wife, a couple of miles out of town. And that they are regarded with some suspicion and hostility because they are different, and keep to themselves.

'I fear that I am going to disappoint many of you, this afternoon, who asked for a service, who came here hoping, and rightfully expecting, to be entertained, perhaps to hear something instructive and worth while. But I can't talk to you in light

116

vein today—or even find anything to say. Not now. For, you see, Amos McGilroy was my foster-father. I am going out there now—to beg their forgiveness, to get right with them and make my peace—if I can.

'If he still wants to shoot me for what I did to him, and most of all to his wife, my mother—and no man ever had a better mother—then that is his right, and I will not raise a hand to stop him! Though I hope for their pardon. Tonight—if I get it—perhaps I can have something to say to you that may be worth listening to.'

He finished and stood for a moment, while the only sound was the buzzing of flies in a shaft of sunlight. Then he turned to step down. But now, before his own startled gaze and the staring eyes of the others, Amos McGilroy was raising up again— crawling for a second time out from underneath the platform.

His lean, sunken cheeks were covered with a several days' growth of beard, his white hair, thin and unkempt, had known no comb of late. There was dried blood on his face, a deep gash in the right cheek, and he was an almost frightening apparition. But, transfiguringly enough, he was smiling, and tears were running down his cheeks.

'Jim!' he said. 'Jim, boy!'

He staggered as he tried to climb up onto the platform, and Gentleman Jim sprang and caught him, then for a moment they were clasped in each other's arms. Happy, watching, thought that he was beginning to understand some of the ferment working in his friend.

Presently the old man turned, looking out at the still silent audience, and his voice rang clear.

'I have a word to say to ye! Never did I think to address such a gatherin' as this, and most especial you here in this town, whom I've had scant liking for—as I know ye have for me in turn! And yet—here I am, because here stands me boy, come back to us by the grace of the good Lord!

''Tis the truth he's told, today—every word is God's truth! There was black hate in me heart, as there has been for years. Hate for him, and for me fellow men—almost for the good God above us and all things else! There has been hate in me heart and little of love or goodness since that day when this boy ran away. Yesterday I came here to kill him, havin' discovered who he was, but I was too slow. I was thrown out, and I cut me cheek on a rock as I fell, and me hate grew the blacker. I would not allow even me good wife to wash the blood away when she felt it there—that was a part of me hate, for him, and for every one of ye! For today I was going to kill ye, every one! There was even those who wanted to

118

*hire* me to do the work of vengeance!'

He paused a moment, and there was nothing fanatical in his eyes now, but they could not doubt. Then he went on, clinging to Gentleman Jim, his voice more quiet.

'If you will look—and be a bit careful about it—you will find dynamite and fuse and caps set under the platform here now. Enough to blow up this whole place and every man, woman and child in it. Sure, I knew I would die along with the rest of ye, but did not Samson pray for strength to pull down the temple and destroy his enemies, and ask only to die with them? It was in me mind to do the same.'

A tense, shocked hush had fallen now.

'I had but to touch the match to the fuse, and it was in me hand ready to the lightin'. But then he began to talk—and I listened. 'Twas the truth ye told, son—the whole truth—confessin' your mistakes like a man. 'Twas forgiveness ye said ye'd sought—and I find the bitterness gone from me heart and room for love in it ag'in. Ye're mother is blind, boy—blind and crippled, and I—God forgive me—in me own blindness I'd have destroyed meself and all the rest and left her to perish without me to care for her!

'But come along now, for never did the hate crowd out the love in her heart! She is as ever she was, a saint upon this earth, and waiting    only    to    welcome    her    boy back—though she knows not that you are here, for should I tell her anything to add to her grief? But now we need wait no longer. So, me son, come on home! The light is still in the window!'

## CHAPTER THIRTEEN

## TEN-SPOT LOLO

The banker's carriage was waiting as Gentleman Jim came out of the tent with Amos McGilroy. Maita Gilson was holding the reins, keeping the impatient team from too much fretting. Her hand upon the lines, her low voice in an occasional word, seemed to have the power to soothe the sorrels, to turn their capering into a playful display.

'You'll want this,' she suggested, and handed the reins to Gentleman Jim as she got out. He took them, thanking her with his eyes, while the old man turned to look at her with gaze suddenly keen, then he lifted his battered hat gravely before climbing over the wheel.

''Tis a great man ye have become, Jim,' he said. 'It's proud of ye I am this day.'

The evening shadows were lengthening, the last splash of the sunset fading out like a lingering benediction, when the team and

120

buggy came back to town and the big tent. Already it was filled, with the crowd patiently waiting. Happy, fighting against an ever-growing nervousness, was playing softly. He had discovered that there was a soothing effect to some of these old songs. That was what he needed, more than did his listeners.

If there had been a feeling of disaster in the air before, it was more than that now. Gentleman Jim was a contrary man. Happy knew that. Usually he turned his contrariness against others, but this time he had stubbornly set it against himself.

'There'll be fireworks,' Happy muttered under his breath. 'Sure as blazes. And us right in the middle. Next thing, he'll be tellin' them what we come here for, and beggin' their pardon for it. I should be makin' tracks for somewhere else, but what the blazes!'

Gentleman Jim entered the tent, carrying his foster-mother in his arms. Nora McGilroy was a frail little lady, her hair a silver crown, the eyes under it so bright as to belie the notion that sight was gone from them. It might have been the day and what it had meant, but she seemed vivid and almost youthful as he placed her on one of the front benches and padded it with a blanket. For a moment she clung to his hand.

'Jim, boy,' she whispered. 'Sure and ye've made me a happy woman this night! Never did I think that you were this great Professor! What you have to say I shall enjoy!'

'I hope so, Mother,' Gentleman Jim agreed quietly, and stood looking down at her for a moment. There was a battle ahead, in this town—he had no doubt of that, nor fear of it. Such things he had met before. But he had somewhat the same feeling as bothered Happy.

Amos McGilroy came hurrying in, breathless, to take his place beside his wife. He was a transformed man from the dishevelled creature of the afternoon. Washed and shaved, neatly dressed, his neighbours stared covertly.

'Friends,' Gentleman Jim said, when he stood up to speak, 'I guess you know without telling that there are a lot of things which I might say to you, and I expect that you're curious—and rightly so. But I'll have to leave some things to your imagination and the fact, which I've discovered, that you're neighbourly folks, and understanding.

'So that's what I want to talk to you about tonight—neighbourliness. Everybody working together, to build a better community. And it takes everybody, if we're going to have things as they should be. You

122

ladies know that when you make bread, it takes only a little yeast to make over a whole big batch of dough. A mighty small patch in the whole—but important. And a cinder in the eye can make a man miserable.'

Another man had quietly taken his seat near the rear of the tent. Ten-Spot Lolo, who had first come here to kill him. Gentleman Jim saw him, but he went on as though this was just another man who had come to listen.

'Before a man can see straight, or feel like himself, he's got to get rid of that cinder. Here in Hangman's Coulee we've had quite a bit of talk, but talk isn't enough. We've got to have action as well, to get rid of our cinders. And it'll hurt while we do it. But not half so much as trying to get along with them.'

He went on, developing his theme. As usual, once he warmed to his topic, there was an impelling earnestness to him which held his auditors. He concluded, looking down at them in silence for a minute. Then he spoke again.

'I'm not talking like a professor tonight—or showing you any slides. But sometimes things get too big for us—unless we rope and tie and brand them before they get out of control. This afternoon, Amos McGilroy said that my mother had always kept a light in the window—for me. Well, there's a light for all of us to follow, and a job to be done. I'd like to know how many of you want to make a better town here, a better community. And how many are willing to stand up and be counted?'

There were startled, uneasy looks on some faces. He wasn't asking much, but it meant taking sides. But several were on their feet, promptly, then others, until most of the audience was standing. Among the first to stand was Ten-Spot Lolo.

'Reckon you're in the right of it, Professor,' he said. 'Time something was done here. I'm with you.'

There was a vociferous chorus from others, and the meeting broke up. Gentleman Jim knew that he should have been elated, but he was puzzled and depressed instead. The feeling persisted during the drive out to the McGilroy cabin, where he lingered briefly promising to return the next day.

He was nearly back to town when the horses shied. Something was there, at the side of the road, an object darker than the rest. A man, sprawled with arms wide flung, face half-hidden in the grass and rotting leaves of yesteryear. Only as he reached him did Gentleman Jim recognize Ten-Spot.

For a moment he drew back in horror, then forced himself to touch him. There was blood, half-dried, still ebbing from a small round hole almost between the shoulder blades, soaking the shirt and dripping to the ground. But Ten-Spot was still alive.

The creek was not far off, and taking Ten-Spot's big hat, Gentleman Jim brought water and held it to his lips, partly raising him. Ten-Spot stirred as it trickled into his mouth, choked and swallowed. His eyes stared on vacancy, pain-filled. Then, as he recognized the face bending above him, light came into his own.

'It's you—Professor,' he whispered. 'I was hopin'—to have a little talk with you. Come out this way—for that. And to kind of—'

'Better not do any talking just now,' Gentleman Jim advised. He was soaking a handkerchief, wadding it above the wound to staunch the bleeding. 'I'll get you in to a doctor quick as we can travel.'

'Reckon I've got too bad a hole in me—for that,' Ten-Spot protested. 'And anyway, it don't matter. I—'

'I'm going to take you in now,' Gentleman Jim said, gathering the injured man up in his arms. 'We'll take care of you, Ten-Spot. Did you see who it was that shot you?'

'No. I didn't know anybody was after me—thought it was just you they had it in for. I was thinkin' about the things you said—cleanin' out the bad spots—'

## CHAPTER FOURTEEN

# QUITE AN IDEA

Having placed Ten-Spot in the doctor's care, Gentleman Jim sought out the sheriff. This was a new role for him. Usually it had been the other way around. But tonight he was thinking of the injured man, not of himself. It occurred to him, wryly, that lately he had been thinking along strange lines. Much more so than of the business which had brought him to Hangman's Coulee.

Sheriff Hoffman listened to his recital without comment. Gentleman Jim could almost read the thoughts passing in his mind. Ten-Spot Lolo was not a man to lose any sleep over, even if the wound which he had taken should prove fatal. There were too many of his sort around for one to be missed. Indeed, a general cleaning out, by whatever method, might be all to the good.

'You any idea who shot him?' Hoffman asked.

'I could hazard a guess,' Gentleman Jim replied. 'And so could you, I expect.'

The sheriff shrugged, his eyes veiled.

'Guessing's no good,' he retorted. 'I've made a lot of guesses in my day—some of

126

'em wrong. Or are you guessin' the same as I am?'

'How do you mean?'

'Somebody might have figured that you had gone that way, Professor—but without knowin' that you were driving. You've got a habit of hiking around after dark on foot. No tellin' how many have noticed it.'

'You're observant,' Gentleman Jim said drily.

'Pays to be, in my place. But, like I say, I ain't the only one. You got plenty folks interested in you, some for one reason, some for another. Suppose somebody mistook Ten-Spot for you. In the dark, you look a lot alike. I'm just guessin', you understand.'

Gentleman Jim pondered that. It could be, of course. In fact, Ten-Spot himself had hinted as much. Hoffman asked the same question which had been put to him before.

'You pack a gun, Professor?'

Gentleman Jim shook his head.

'It hardly seems in keeping with my calling, Sheriff.'

'That's a matter of opinion, too,' the sheriff said ambiguously. 'But seems like you're makin' yourself right unpopular around here, considerin' how short a time you've been in town.'

That remark held room for thought, some of it depressing. But Gentleman Jim was closer to his old, devil-may-care mood than he had been since coming to town. The events of the day had given him a lift, and if there was a fight, he was never one to dodge it. That was a relief from thinking of his own problems.

There was no change in Ten-Spot's condition the next morning. It would be close, the doctor reported, whichever way it went. Ten-Spot was in a half-coma, but he was suffering no pain.

At least, there was plenty to do, and Jim needed something to work at. The little cabin occupied by his foster-parents was neat and clean, but it had been bare to the point of bleakness. He hitched the team to the covered wagon and drove around to Sam Staves' General Merchandise Emporium, and began to order, carrying out the goods until the wagon was filled with a wide variety of items. Staves and Happy assisted him, and in the midst of the job, Staves startled him with an offhand remark.

'You ain't been chargin' no admission, nor takin' up no collections at the lectures, Professor,' he pointed out.

'No,' Gentleman Jim agreed. And added, by way of explanation. 'I thought I'd better give something worth their money, first.'

'You been doing that, and folks would feel better about it,' Staves said. 'You ought to be paid. And Gilson has got a new notion. Spoke to me about it last evenin'. He said anything to you yet?'

'No. Is it important?'

'Seems so to us.' Staves chuckled. 'I don't suppose it meant anything to you, but there was a lady stood up at your call last night—wore a calico dress and high-behind comb and all. She and her husband are from the Antler. One of the best an' biggest outfits in this part of the country. And the point is, when Samantha says something, Mose Kearney comes like a calf when its ma bellers. Mose, he's a tough hombre, and proud of it. But he knows who's boss.'

'What you gettin' at, Sam?' Happy demanded. Gentleman Jim noted that the two were 'Sam' and 'John' to one another now. Which was not surprising, considering how much time Happy spent at the Staves' house.

'Just this,' Staves chuckled. 'Mose, and Samantha, too, they been tighter'n the bark on a November tree. Got a wad of money, but they hang onto it same's a cocklebur to a horse's tail. But if Samantha gets interested, and you point out the need for funds, she'll likely make Mose loosen up. They didn't contribute a cent to the railroad fund, but no reason why they shouldn't give generous to some good project.'

'Now that's an idea!' Happy interjected, and glanced obliquely at Gentleman Jim.

129

'Er—what did you have in mind?' Gentleman Jim asked.

'It's Gilson's notion that we ought to raise money and build us a church and get a sky pilot in here,' Staves explained. 'Kind of keep folks in the right frame of mind, after you get 'em prepared.'

*A church!* Gentleman Jim thought, startled. *No wonder Hathaway's getting scared and vindictive!* But his comment was quite enough.

'Sounds like quite an idea.'

'Yeah. Gilson has it in mind that we'd ought to keep up the good work. Not just sort of brand a bunch of mavericks and then leave 'em to run wild again. There's always plenty chance for strayin', that way—even to gettin' their brand vented and the wrong iron on 'em again. So why not take up a collection or so, he was sayin' to me, and use it for buildin' a church?'

'The idea has possibilities,' Gentleman Jim conceded, observing again the flame in Happy's eyes.

'Yeah. Well, if you're agreeable, why not take a collection for that tonight?' Staves asked. 'Ought to get a nice start toward what's needed, and before these meetings are over, we'll have plenty rounded up to do the job. Make this a town to amount to something, while we're about it. What do you think, Maita?'

130

'I think it's a wonderful idea,' Maita Gilson agreed. She had come up while they talked, and now she surveyed the loaded wagon, then turned to Gentleman Jim with a dawning smile. 'You're taking these things out to your folks?'

'Why—why, yes, I was figuring on it,' Gentleman Jim agreed. 'It looks like they could use a few things—and I've been neglecting them so long—'

For almost the first time since she had met him, he was ill at ease, and she thought she knew why.

'It hasn't been your fault—not since you found yourself,' she pointed out. 'You're doing all that you can now to make up for it.'

'I aim to do what I can,' Gentleman Jim agreed, and wondered how much he could do, or how long he would have a chance to do it in. Events were getting out of hand. A man could scratch a match to light a fire, but in dry grass it could become a devouring monster.

'Would you like to go along out there with me?' he asked. And that, like a lot of other things which he had said of late, seemed to be voiced outside his own volition. It was a question which immediately left him fearing what the answer might be.

But her retort was prompt and decisive.

'I'd love to. I was hoping you'd asked me.'

The sun seemed suddenly warmer, the sky bluer. As he assisted her up to the wagon seat and then swung up himself, the old lines came to his mind. *What is so rare as a day in June!* He grinned to himself. *And I never thought too much of June, before!*

Happy, watching them drive away, shook his head, grinning in turn. His face had lost a lot of its dourness in the last few days.

'Figured I'd have to go along and do the heavy work,' he commented. 'Unloadin' all that stuff. Guess I'm not needed now, the way it looks.'

'You'd just be in the way,' Staves agreed. 'But if you were to go out to the house now, I'll bet Minerva would be glad to see you. She was tellin' me she'd never realized how lonesome it got around there, till you started droppin' in.'

'Reckon I'll do that, then,' Happy decided. 'I was just tryin' to figure out some good excuse.'

It was Staves' turn to grin.

'When a man wants to do something that somebody else wants him to do,' he said sagely, 'what does he need of an excuse?'

\*　　\*　　\*

The McGilroys were speechless at sight of

132

the load which Gentleman Jim delivered. There were groceries, blankets, a rocking chair, a new coal-oil lamp, and as wide a variety in between as the store had been able to provide. They were busy for some time, carrying the things in and arranging or putting them away. Maita put on the teapot, at Nora McGilroy's request, for a 'sip of tay' all around. Gentleman Jim observed that the two women, the one old and sightless, the other young and from an environment entirely different, were much alike at heart. They seemed to take to each other.

'Sure, and I know now that the Lord's in His heaven,' Amos McGilroy said fervently. 'Though 'tis not in answer to anything I have done that this has come about—'twill be the prayers of Nora and her faith when me own was runnin' out like a spring freshet down the gully. But one thing has troubled me, Jim boy,' he added. 'In town here you're known as Timothy Meader. Which is not your name.'

'No,' Gentleman Jim agreed, 'it's not my name. But I stopped using that—a long while ago. The same as I never used your name. At least, I didn't drag them in the dust.'

'There's sure to be dust along any road that we travel far,' Nora commented. 'Which don't stop the grass from growing

133

green beside it, or the flowers on the hillsides showin' as pretty as a new patchwork quilt. Also, it's surprising how quick a shower can wash away the dust.'

'I begin to see where you gained the inspiration for some of the beautiful thoughts which you have in your lectures,' Maita said softly.

'That's right,' Gentleman Jim agreed. 'I never realized before, myself. But now it's easy to see.'

'Sho', go on with your blarney, the both of you!' Nora's cheeks were colouring like a schoolgirl's. Then, as they stood up to go, she took one of Maita's hands in both of hers and held it for a moment.

''Tis a fine, strong hand, and sure,' she said. 'And from that I know what you're like. Belike the good Lord had more than one reason for guiding you to this town, Jim boy. You'll come to see me again, Maita?'

'I'd love to,' the girl agreed warmly.

'Which makes it mutual. See that ye bring her then, Jim.' And as they drove away, Gentleman Jim was conscious that Nora was standing beside her husband, waving to them with a certainty of vision which went beyond mere physical sight.

## CHAPTER FIFTEEN

# MURDER

For an hour or so, with Maita beside him and the visit to pay, Jim had been able to forget; or at least to push other and less pleasant thoughts aside. Back in town that was no longer possible. Ten-Spot Lolo was dead. And while it was probable, as the sheriff had pointed out, that the bullet which had struck him down had been intended for Gentleman Jim himself, the result in any case was murder.

A murder which must go unavenged—unless he did something about it! And everything which he did seemed to be driving him to work against himself, against the objectives which had brought him to this community in the first place.

But this was just one added item among those piling up like a snowdrift before the wind. His coming to this town had been the trigger to unloose a conflict which had been in the making for a long while.

Hardly had he returned when he had a caller. Jake Elliott was no long-faced, sedate undertaker. He was a plump, red-faced man, always ready to crack a joke and grave only when professional duty demanded. Life and death, to him, were everyday matters to be taken as they came. In the passing of Ten-Spot Lolo he saw nothing to regret.

'Only thing is, Professor, I want to get this straight,' he explained. 'Somebody was tellin' me that Ten-Spot had stood up and sort of put himself on your side, at the meetin' the other night. Which, as Bob was sayin', is about the same thing for him as if he'd gone and got religion. I couldn't rightly believe any change of Ten-Spot, if 'twasn't that I used to watch tadpoles change to frogs, or these kind of ugly grubs wrap themselves up in cocoons and come out butterflies the next summer. Purty as a calf's ear, too, some of 'em. Anyway, since Ten-Spot made the change, and you're in town, I suppose we got to start thinkin' of doing different from what we used to. Since we ain't got no parson, and you're easy with words, you might want to say a few words over Ten-Spot, eh? Be a big change from the words that's mostly been said about him these late years.'

'I think that's what he'd want,' Gentleman Jim agreed, remembering the dying man when he had lifted him in his arms. Here was one more job that he had not counted on. But it should not be too hard to manage.

'Sure thing,' Elliott agreed cheerfully. 'When'll suit you best for the job? Want it now, or later?'

'How about Sunday afternoon? I'm going to be pretty busy, the rest of today and tomorrow. And there's no rush.'

Jake Elliott eyed him shrewdly.

'Sure, Sunday'll be as good as any time,' he nodded. 'Might be a lot bigger occasion by then, too, eh? Never can tell.'

Gentleman Jim was not quite sure why he had put it off. Save that he felt unsure of himself. He rejected John Gilson's suggestion that an offering be taken at the afternoon lecture, to go to himself, but agreed to one that evening toward the new church. Gilson explained to the crowd what they intended to do, and the purpose for which the money was intended. Heads nodded in approval. Staves made a comment, at the end of the afternoon meeting.

'Ought to get money enough, out of this crowd, to build the church, in one collection,' he said. 'They've got it— and they're in a mood to be gen'rous, looks like. You're really mellowin' 'em up, Professor.'

Happy gave him a sidelong glance as they returned to their room.

'You're workin' it smart, Jim,' he said. 'For a while you had me guessin'. But this way, one thing and another, we'll make a big clean-up.'

Gentleman Jim turned miserably.

'Suppose we don't make a clean-up, Happy?' he challenged.

Happy nodded soberly.

'I know what you mean,' he agreed. 'I'm thinkin' some of Minerva. Anything you do, Jim—it'll be all right with me.'

'That's the devil of it,' Gentleman Jim confessed savagely. 'You're in this—and people like the Gilsons and the Staves, not to mention any others. No matter what we do, this is going to hurt them, before it's over with.' He eyed Happy sharply. 'You could get out now, if you wanted to,' he added.

Happy shook his head.

'It don't look too good,' he confessed. 'Still, I've seen it look plenty bad before. I remember one time, a mob of folks started to lynch me. But I'm still alive.'

'That big tree is still standing.'

Happy shivered.

'Yeah,' he agreed. 'I can see it every time I look out—or even when I shut my eyes. I even dream about it, and wake up sweatin'.' He closed his eyes tightly, opened them again. 'But you're in this up to the neck, Jim,' he added stubbornly. 'And long as you stay, I aim to stick, too.'

Neither of them discussed the other implications. There seemed no point in doing so. Events were getting beyond control, like a rock rolling down hill.

Gentleman Jim lectured abstractedly that evening, sticking to the lantern slides for the occasion. He explained then about the collection, and watched while it was being taken. Only when it was over with did he sense that something was wrong.

Many in the audience seemed to understand that, too, as though they had been aware of trouble from the start. Gilson, Boggs and Staves were conferring over the hats which had been passed and emptied again. Then Samantha Kearney approached, her husband in tow. Samantha was small and frail beside her two-fisted husband, but tonight their roles seemed to be reversed. He was shrinking and ill at ease, while she folded her arms and stood like an attorney for the prosecution.

'Collection way off from what you thought it'd be, or what it ought to be, eh?' she demanded.

Staves eyed her shrewdly.

'It's a bit disappointing, for a fact,' he conceded. 'Not hardly enough to jingle.'

Samantha snorted.

'I knew it!' she said triumphantly. 'And I'm ashamed of this big walrus! I told him, when a collection came up, and for a church at that, that he was to put in a thousand dollars! We ain't never been what you'd call church-goers—don't know that we'd be, even if there was a church within a hundred miles. But it's the principle of the thing. He could easy afford the money—if he hadn't gone and made a ring-tailed fool of himself! Like a lot of other men I could mention!'

'Aw, now, Ma—' Mose Kearney protested, weakly.

'Don't you "Aw, now, Ma," me!' Samantha retorted indignantly. 'Do you know how much he put in that hat? One dollar! One measly little coin. And why? Because he'd been over to Deal Hathaway's saloon and gambled all the rest that he had with him when we come to town! Lost it! Five thousand dollars, in a few hours—like a lot of other fools!'

Gentleman Jim pricked up his ears. Five thousand dollars! He knew that Hathaway had gotten in a couple of wagonloads of new gambling equipment, since he and Happy had come to town, and that it had created a lot of interest. But tales of such games had somehow not been relayed to him. It was so big as to be staggering.

Samantha Kearney swung to face him.

'That's what's happened, Professor,' she added. 'Shows we need a church, like Mr. Gilson and some of them think. But that ain't the worst! Everybody that goes to play is being cheated, over at the hell-hole! Though the men ain't got the gumption to say it themselves, or to face that black-hearted Deal Hathaway! He's killed

140

men before, to say nothing of the crew of gunmen he keeps at heel! But *I* say it! He's running crooked games there. How else could everybody be losing, the way it's happening?'

She glared around, but no one voiced a denial. Plainly they shared the same opinion.

'It's bad enough for us to lose that much money,' she went on. 'But we can afford it—and we'll dig up as much for the church as you got cheated out of by being a fool, Mose Kearney! Don't think but what you will! I've helped you scrimp and pinch and save all these years, and worn duds that a scarecrow'd be ashamed to be seen wearin' in a cornfield, and gone without—till we're rich! And said nothing about it—at least not much! But when I drag you to town here to listen to the Professor and to get something decent into you, and the first thing you do is go and make a fool of yourself by gambling—only that it ain't even that—'

For a moment she breathed heavily, scarcely able to control herself. Then went on, more calmly.

'Like I say, we'll make it good, for that's only fair, and a needed lesson—maybe for both of us, for being such grubbing fools so long! When you talked tonight, Professor, I looked up and saw stars—really saw 'em, I guess, for the first time in years. We can

141

afford that money!

'But the pity of it is that there's others that can't. Like Nobel Cutting, in off that homestead at the edge of Lonesome, with his wife! They scrimp because they have to! Going to have a baby. Came in to these meetings, and with a hundred dollars above the mortgage that they owe Dan Redding. Five hundred to Dan, a hundred to get a new dress for Mary and a few clothes for the baby! And what does Nobel do, like any noble man when he gets drunk, but go and lose every cent on that crooked wheel today! God knows what they'll do now—starve, I expect!'

Again she paused, breathing hard: Her voice shrilled.

'You talk about community pride, Professor, and making this a better place to live in, and such things as being decent—and the good Lord knows we need it! But what good's lecturin', if that sort of thing goes on at the same time? Oh, I wish I was a man! You're all afraid of Deal Hathaway and his mangy pack of coyotes. But I'm thinkin' of Mary Cutting, and the look on her face—'

She broke off, shaken by sobs. Mose Kearney put an awkward arm about her shoulders.

'There, there, Samantha, gal, don't take on so,' he protested. 'I know I been a

142

fool—a lot of us have. But I—if you feel that way about it, why I—I'll dig out my old gun and go over to that saloon—'

'You'll do nothing of the sort, you old fool,' Samantha protested, clinging to him. 'I guess I talk too much—sometimes. I didn't drag you here just to be killed—at least not till the Professor's softened you up some, and we got a sky pilot and given him a chance to get to that heart of yours, if you've got one down under all the callouses! What chance would you stand over there? What chance does any man in this town stand against Deal Hathaway, if it comes to guns—or anything else? There's never been a man to equal him that way, and don't you think he knows it? Oh—not that, Mose. I didn't bring you here to bury you.'

Others had listened with sympathy, but now they were moving unobtrusively away, the hand of fear upon them as they went. Deal Hathaway had never been bested in a gunfight. But even more to the point, Deal Hathaway had plenty of others to make it unnecessary even for him to draw a gun.

Gentleman Jim had listened. He watched the others depart now, the spirit suddenly gone out of them. Samantha Kearney's words rang in his ears.

'What good's lecturin', if that sort of thing goes on at the same time?'

He turned abruptly, and Happy eyed him

suspiciously.

'Where you goin'?' he demanded.

'I've got some business to attend to,' Gentleman Jim said. 'Business that can't wait!'

## CHAPTER SIXTEEN

## WHITE HANDLES

Happy followed, his own legs racing each other to match the stride set by his friend. Back at their room, Gentleman Jim delved into his duffel bag, and Happy watched morosely. He had no need to ask what was intended. He knew.

Carefully, Gentleman Jim laid aside the garments which he had worn since coming to Hangman's Coulee—the extra suit of sober black which belonged to Timothy Meader. He took an outfit which he had owned for years but had not worn for some time. It still fitted well.

This was strange attire for a sober-minded professor. There had not been too much difference between the broadcloth of Timothy Meader and the usual outfit affected by Gentleman Jim Thornton, but these clothes were not of that class. He donned a fawn-coloured chamois

144

shirt, then a blue suit, light enough in colour to match the daytime skies outside, but with a fine pin stripe running through it. A wide-brimmed grey hat and a red necktie made the transformation almost complete.

What was lacking came when he buckled on a cartridge belt with twin holsters. The guns with which he filled these were regulation Colts save for one detail. They had white handles—of bone, not ivory. Ivory was well enough for gamblers and tenderfeet who thought more of display than of the serious side of their business. When Gentleman Jim had purchased these guns he had given attention to both. Bone handles would not grow slippery under a man's moist palms, as ivory might.

Thoughtfully he twirled the cylinders, then glanced up to meet Happy's gaze.

'They're mostly bluff, Happy,' he exclaimed softly. 'As I think I mentioned once before, I've never killed a man—and I never intend to.'

'But I mind how you blew the gun out of a killer's hand, once, and another time you shot the trigger finger off before a lightnin' fast jasper could get it where he wanted it,' Happy grunted. 'In any case, I wouldn't want no truck with you—not with guns. And most folks don't know that you wouldn't be shootin' to kill.'

'That,' Gentleman Jim sighed, 'may be

one point in our favour.'

Happy shook his head.

'You're going in there lookin' for trouble,' he said. 'And you'll sure find it! But them others—the crew that Hathaway keeps to back him up—*they* won't have no scruples about shootin' to kill!'

'That,' Gentleman Jim murmured, as he stood in front of the mirror and carefully knotted the tie, 'could be what they call a blessing in disguise.'

'Meanin' that you'd just as soon they packed you out, first feet?'

'It would resolve a lot of questions.'

'The devil it would,' Happy growled. 'For you, maybe. But how about this town?'

Gentleman Jim considered him.

'That seems to be the point, doesn't it? I come here to get paid by the town—and this is what happens. I don't know what's happened to me, Happy. I've never gotten into a jam like this before. But, as to your question, I would hope, in that eventuality, to resolve at least some of those questions at the same time.'

'Huh? But how about me? How about Miss Maita? Or ain't you thinkin' about her none?'

'What right have I to think about her—or anything that's fine and decent?' Gentleman Jim demanded bitterly. He clapped on his hat, turned.

146

'All that I'm thinking of, right now, is a job that has to be done,' he sighed. 'This seems to be the most fitting attire to do it in. Are you coming?'

'What else'd I be taggin' along for? That ain't goin' to be no health resort. And if too many others try and horn in—well, I can still use a gun pretty good myself.'

That was rank understatement, as Gentleman Jim knew. If there was a faster man on the draw in this town than Deal Hathaway—not counting himself—then there was small doubt as to where the honours would go. He paused for a moment to clap his smaller companion on the back.

'Happy,' he said. 'I think I've been overlooking a bet for quite a while. There's a lot more to you than I used to think.'

'Not so much to make a target as you,' Happy grunted, and lifted one eyebrow. 'Ain't you going to shock folks? Seein' their Professor, wearin' that get-up?'

'Sometimes you don't mind a hard jolt quite so much if you've had a smaller kick first, to kind of prepare the way,' Gentleman Jim retorted, and, outside in the night, led the way directly.

There was no moon overhead. Clouds had overspread the heavens, and there was a feel of rain in the air. Happy sniffed.

''Bout time for the June rains to be settin' in,' he prophesied. 'Our spell of good

147

weather is near played out.'

'It's been a long spring,' Gentleman Jim said sententiously, and was silent. They reached the big saloon and let themselves in. The Cattleman's was filled almost to capacity tonight, its lights garish. There had been a change here since Gentleman Jim's first visit.

Those wagonloads of new equipment had made a difference. All along one wall they ran, opposite the bar. The games were still spangled with garish new paint, and their novelty in the eyes of the crowd had not worn off. The ugly rumours which were being whispered about the town kept few players from trying these new toys. Perhaps because a certain number of men won. There always had to be come-ons for the suckers.

No one noticed them at first. Then someone recognized Happy, and a moment later, goggling a bit, they knew the tall stranger beside him. A shocked murmur went about the room when they saw the Professor and viewed his fancy garb and the low-slung weapons at his hips. There was an artificial quality to the conversation as it resumed, as though now they were waiting for something to happen.

Gentleman Jim strolled toward one of the roulette wheels. A momentary hush descended upon the room, and he saw that

Deal Hathaway had just emerged from his office. Someone had lost no time in taking the word to him.

Disregarding him, Gentleman Jim eyed the still spinning wheel. These were the first games of this sort ever to make their appearance in Hangman's Coulee, and he could well understand the fascination which they exerted on those who liked to wager money. Outwardly, they looked pretty, sleek and dangerous, and they were all of that.

Deal Hathaway paused indecisively, then veered off toward the bar. Probably he had aimed to speak to the Professor. But this gambler wearing twin six-guns was an unknown quantity, so now he had decided to wait and see what happened.

Gentleman Jim had seen enough already. These wheels were an old story to him. He had worked similar ones himself, on the Barbary Coast. Just long enough to learn their secrets, for he had prided himself on being a straight gambler. And there was nothing straight about such a wheel as this.

The dealer sat close to it. He had to, to work the device which tilted the running wheel to suit his fancy and the convenience of the house. Gentleman Jim hesitated. He could denounce the wheels and the man who owned them, overturn this one and show the crowd how it worked. That would be one way of doing.

To do that would finish Deal Hathaway. It would be a gun-smoke finish, or, if he lived long enough, a final act out at the Tree. Other men would almost certainly be killed as well, before the smoke settled.

But there might be another and possibly better way of doing. There could be no sure way of knowing about that, until all the returns were in. But at least it would be more to his liking.

The players about this wheel glanced up nervously. Sight of the Professor in such guise was warning enough. Now they were leaving their chairs, not liking it, scenting trouble. Gentleman Jim shifted one chair and sat down. Seated so, he was close to the dealer—close enough that he not only faced him directly, but so that it would be impossible for the fellow to operate the secret mechanism.

Happy had moved across to the wall and placed his back to it. From that point he could command the room, if necessity arose. No gunman could get behind him—or behind Gentleman Jim, while he was there to watch. And this move was not lost on Deal Hathaway.

'I think I'll try the red six,' Gentleman Jim murmured, and laid down a handful of silver. He took the chips which the dealer shoved uncertainly across to him, palming them with the skill of long practice. He placed ten of them on the red as the wheel spun, and by now most of the other games in the room were deserted. The crowd was watching him, openly or covertly.

The wheel rolled straight and true, hesitated, came to a stop. If Gentleman Jim felt any surprise, his face did not betray it. The dealer gazed at it blankly.

'Red six wins,' he croaked.

Deal Hathaway appeared beside him. He was smiling, but nervousness showed in the pin-points of his eyes.

'Well, well, Professor,' he said heartily. 'Welcome to our entertainment! Or should I call you Professor?'

'I've been called worse things than that, and probably will be again,' Gentleman Jim retorted. 'However, I'm not here strictly as a professor tonight. Or if so, as one in an inquiring frame of mind. I've heard it said that these wheels of yours are crooked, Hathaway. So I thought I'd see for myself.'

Sudden silence had fallen on the room at the blunt charge. Hathaway's face lost its colour, then he smiled.

'Then I take it that you consider yourself an expert on the subject—of crooked wheels?' The sneer in his voice was plain. Gentleman Jim nodded, unperturbed.

'I do,' he agreed. 'As I think I've indicated before, I haven't always been a professor.'

'A lot of people might be right int'rested to know what you *have* been,' Deal Hathaway suggested, and the malice was unhidden.

'They might, at that,' Gentleman Jim conceded. His eyes rested lightly on the pressing crowd, gauging those who were gun hirelings. Probably half a dozen of them, at least. Which was about the way he had expected it.

'I'll give the red six another ride—just for luck.' He shoved his winnings back on it, watching the wheel spin with no show of emotion. 'For any who may be interested, I will say this much. I am here to do two things. To see for myself whether or not there is any foundation to those charges of crooked games in this place. And, in the process of testing them, to get back, if I may, the losses sustained by certain ill-advised players who could not afford to lose. If luck is with me, I propose to return their money to them—to such men as Nobel Cutting.'

'Red six wins,' the dealer intoned, but his voice had lost its calmness. This was beginning to look like a run of luck. Like most men of his profession, he had a deadly fear of a run. Particularly when he could not manipulate the wheel to control it.

Absently, Gentleman Jim accepted the winnings. Every man in the room was

152

watching now, none attempting to disguise their interest.

'If you don't mind, Hathaway, I think I'll take cash instead of chips,' Gentleman Jim suggested. 'It will save trouble.'

'Of course,' Hathaway agreed readily, but now the sneer was back in his voice. 'Through so soon? Or are you satisfied that the wheel's straight?'

'Neither,' Gentleman Jim retorted. 'I just prefer cash—so long as you have any.'

Deal Hathaway went a little paler than habitual, at the unmistakable threat in the words. He knew, no man better, how quickly the game or the house could be broken or a man cleaned out on a run of luck on such a wheel as this. There had been no risk of that sort before, but like his dealer, he had a superstitious fear of what might be beginning now, with this cold-eyed professor playing the red. And, like the dealer, he knew how risky it would be to try and control the wheel. He had a conviction that Gentleman Jim knew what he was talking about when he discussed such matters.

The money was brought, bills and gold eagles, in substitution for the chips. Gentleman Jim accepted it, glanced inquiringly at the dealer, and as the wheel spun again, placed his bet.

Hathaway watched with a face which

gradually showed the strain, as the Professor continued to win. Once or twice he lost, but it seemed almost as if he could pick a winner at will. Occasionally he varied the play, but mostly he stuck to the same colour and combinations. And now this run of luck—for that was what it unmistakably was—was beginning to affect everyone in the room. Gentleman Jim alone seemed unimpressed.

He glanced from Hathaway to the dealer, and as the wheel spun again, placed his bet.

'I'll put everything I have here on it,' he decided. 'And risk the red six again. It seems to be lucky tonight.'

Again it was a win. His face still without expression, Gentleman Jim made a slight variation. He stopped to count off six hundred dollars, and thrust it into a pocket of his shirt.

'That will take care of Cutting,' he explained. 'And the mortgage and the baby. We'll let the rest ride.'

'Red six again?' Hathaway demanded hoarsely.

Gentleman Jim studied him, looked across at the dealer. Then, as the wheel spun, he placed his bet.

'We'll give the black a chance this time.'

And this time it was the black which won. Hathaway's face looked sunken and old, but, becoming aware that everybody was

154

watching him, he shrugged and moved carelessly away.

'You're quite a show, Professor,' he called back, with emphasis on the last word. 'But even you should be satisfied by now that the wheel is straight. Neither fools, professors nor professional gamblers could better such a run—particularly on a crooked wheel.'

'Sometimes a crooked wheel has its advantages,' Gentleman Jim murmured. 'This time, we'll return to our first love and the red six,' he added, and indicated his entire winnings as the bet again. The onlookers gasped. He was pyramiding fast now, already with several thousands before him. A couple more such plays, if they won, could break the bank.

Deal Hathaway came back, nervous as a boogery steer. The dealer hesitated, looking to him for instructions. Hathaway scowled, but he could give no orders, not quite sure in his own mind what they would be in any case.

'It may be,' Gentleman Jim remarked thoughtfully, 'that there is a purpose in my winning tonight, that I'm being used just to place the bets. Maybe you've been a thorn in the flesh of this community too long, Hathaway. If I win what you have, tonight, it will be no skill of mine, nor mere luck, but something bigger, before which crooked wheels or straight—or man himself, is a

155

mere novice.' He kept a straight face, speaking as the Professor, but remembering that such talk would have its effect on such men as were before him. Gamblers were superstitious.

'If I should win,' he added, pursuing the same line of logic, 'I shall keep none of it for myself. Not a cent. All will go to the betterment of the community.'

As on other occasions, he shook his head then, startled by what he had just said. Here was a fortune almost within his grasp—a sum which might rival the amount that he had come here to get hold of in the first place. And he was pledging himself not to keep a cent of it!

Of course, he'd been a liar before now, as well as a thief. But the startling thing was that he meant what he was saying. Meant it while he was saying it, at least.

Then, meeting the look on the dealer's face, he was practical again. He moved a little, so that attention was recalled to those twin bone-handled guns which he wore, and the creeping glaze in the dealer's eyes wore itself out. Mechanically he set the wheel to spinning again.

## CHAPTER SEVENTEEN

# LADY LUCK

Whether this was the smile of Lady Luck tonight, or if some more potent force than the mechanism so cleverly concealed in the table guided the wheel, no one was any longer quite sure. Hardened players swore under their breath as the red six won again, and the dealer spoke tonelessly:

'You've busted the bank!'

Deal Hathaway's face had clouded up and greyed with the storm in the last few minutes. He spoke thickly.

'You've got the devil's own luck tonight!'

Gentleman Jim looked at him.

'Now there's a thought,' he murmured. 'One which seems to have a familiar ring. Are you all through, Hathaway?'

'Through?' Stormy colour replaced the pallor. 'I'll show you whether I'm through or not—word-shark!' He leaned forward, thrusting his face close to Gentleman Jim's, and the mask was worn thin. 'I didn't ask you to come here—but if you're looking for something, you can have it. This saloon and the rest of what's in it is equal to all you've won. *If* you want to wager!'

'Why not?' Gentleman Jim asked. 'It's

157

your loss, not mine.'

It was curious. Ordinarily, there was tense excitement in him at such a moment, but now Gentleman Jim felt only indifference. There was nothing to worry about. It would go one way or the other, and results would follow according to the turn of the wheel. Almost he felt sorry for Deal Hathaway, who was doing the sweating.

Happy crouched back against the wall. There was none of the coolness in him that his big partner showed now. Danger was here, and he was acutely aware of it. More than that, there was whisky—row on row of bottles on the shelves behind the bar. The smell of it was in his nostrils, and it was a tantalizing fragrance, stirring old appetites, almost driving him frantic.

Once more the wheel was spinning. Gentleman Jim did not watch it. His eyes were upon the dealer, who was torn between two fears. One was of his employer, if he allowed this man to win again. It had been a long run of luck, and it seemed wild to suppose that the red six would come up again. If he just let it go by itself, Gentleman Jim must surely lose, and all would be as it had been before.

But if the red six won again, and Deal Hathaway was wiped out—the dealer glared wildly around, and his gaze met the sardonic imps which seemed to look back at him out of the Professor's eyes. From there it roved to those twin guns.

He knew nothing of this man who had come here to upset the town—nothing beyond what was gossip these last few days. Whether he could shoot as well as he played the wheel there was no guessing. But a man who knew the tricks of such a game, who packed a brace of guns, was not one to fool with. The dealer had no desire to learn how well he could use them by challenging him now. And then it was too late. The wheel had slowed of its own accord, stopped—on the red six.

Gentleman Jim stood up and began to gather the money and sort it into stacks. His mind was clear, detached, yet it refused to go beyond the present moment, appalled by the implications of the future.

Colour worked a slow way back into Deal Hathaway's face. He knew now what he was going to do.

'Looks like the saloon is yours, Professor,' he said. 'Though what a word-shark will do with a liquor store and gambling joint is beyond me. Or have you changed your mind about things? Maybe you aim to run it?'

'That's a fair question,' Gentleman Jim admitted. 'And the answer is no.'

'Thought so. Well—for a professor, you're quite a gambler. Or it looks that way.' There was studied insult behind the words. 'You said there was something wrong with that wheel, and I'm inclined to agree with you. Must be warped from the heat, or a bit off kilter somehow, and you had a quick enough eye to see it. I'm not blamin' you for takin' advantage. That's fair, if I wasn't bright enough to see it for myself. Only—a gamble's a gamble. I've got other property in town—put it all together and it will balance up to what you've won. I might as well be cleaned out while I'm about it—or back where I was.'

'Meaning?'

'I'll take you on at poker, two-handed. Winner take all.'

Gentleman Jim nodded.

'I'm agreeable.'

'Maybe you don't understand, Professor. I said winner take all. I meant just that—and I reckon you know what I mean.'

Coldness flowed in Gentleman Jim for a moment. What Deal Hathaway was proposing was that, if he won, he not only recovered his losses, but that Gentleman Jim should quit lecturing and get out of town, as he had suggested before. Leaving Hathaway a clear field in everything.

Those were big stakes. They contained imponderables for which a man could scarcely gamble. Then, looking into the slitted eyes of the gambler, he laughed

160

suddenly and shrugged.

'Why not?' he asked. 'If you want it that way.'

For this, after all, was only preliminary. No matter what way it went, it would not be the final solution. He had guessed that far ahead when he strapped the guns about his waist.

This was a test that had to come. The cards, or their lack, could make no real difference. Only with them he might strip Deal Hathaway of all the property he owned in Hangman's Coulee. Here was a chance at far bigger winnings than he had visualized when he had first decided to come here.

But, curiously, he was not thinking of that. Until Hathaway was cleaned out, the town could not be. And that was what the Professor had come for—even if he hadn't known it when he came. That was what Maita wanted.

A fresh deck of cards was brought, and as they sat down at a table, interest was mounting to the breaking point. No one was leaving, though all other activity had long since ceased.

As Gentleman Jim had known, he was matching wits and skill with a gambler who knew every trick of the cards. A man ruthlessly determined to win. Luck, hitherto mostly on his own side, seesawed now, dividing its favours about equally between them.

The real contest here was one of nerves—or nerve. Gambler though he was, Hathaway was starting to crack. The events of the evening had been too shattering, as he had seen his holdings swept away, increasingly, with each turn of the wheel. The knowledge that this game was not the deciding agent in any case stirred his impatience.

It was in the middle of the fifth hand that he cracked.

'For just a word-shark,' he snarled, 'you're too damned good with the pasteboards!'

Even as he spoke, he flung down his cards, fingers moving with a stabbing speed toward his gun. Gentleman Jim had been watching, not Hathaway's hand, but his eyes. He had known almost to the minute when this was coming, and his own response was not what the gambler was looking for.

Gentleman Jim made no move for his own guns. Instead, he flung his cards, spattering them into the face of Hathaway, blinding and disconcerting him for a moment. That was all the time required. He tipped the table back, shoving it hard into Hathaway's middle, upsetting him on the floor. Before he could recover, Gentleman Jim was stooping above him, twisting the gun away.

For a moment he stared down. Naked hate was in Hathaway's eyes as he sprawled and waited for what he was sure was coming.

'You can get up,' Gentleman Jim said. 'Get up and get out, Hathaway. It would be simpler—so much more so—just to shoot you and be done with it. Only I can't very well do that.'

He turned to the crowd, silent and a little awed—some of them held so by the watchfulness of Happy, who had dragged a chair back to the wall and climbed on it, the better to watch.

'This place is closed,' Gentleman Jim announced. 'You men who work here will continue to receive your wages and will be held responsible for it.'

He gathered up his winnings and went out, trailing the uncertain customers. Happy was still tagging him, strangely silent. But, partly because of the way he had handled it, and in part because he was the Professor, who was held in such high esteem by so many in the town, there had been no other trouble. Not for the moment.

Rain was in his face as he came out, but it was only a passing shower. It would take more than rain to wash away his troubles. The evening had only added one more problem. What should he do with the

163

saloon, with his winnings? He had said what he was going to do with them, but it was not so simple as that.

He had spared Deal Hathaway's life, and that had been a foolish thing to do. Hathaway would not leave town, nor would he take this defeat without another try at retaliation. The fact that Gentleman Jim had let him live would excite no gratitude in the mind of the gambler. Quite the contrary, considering how and where it had been done.

But all of those matters, and what they added up to, were trifles compared to the unrest which tormented Jim. He knew now how much of a fool he had been to come here in this guise. Happy had been right.

He'd aimed to play a part and get well paid for it. But the look in a woman's eyes had changed him. Now he was playing a dual role, both in violent contradiction. And no matter what he did, disaster was sure to follow. He was no professor, no decent or respectable character. Playing the part didn't make it so.

Sooner or later his past would catch up with him. If he wasn't a fool, he'd take his winnings and get out. It was the only thing to do. Only—

Already it was past midnight, which meant that this was Sunday. He was supposed to give a general lecture on

Sunday morning and again in the evening, with a big picnic dinner for everyone to be held in the open during the afternoon, if the weather permitted.

The rain had stopped, and a few stars were showing overhead. It would be good weather, he judged, but none of that really mattered.

'Better come to bed,' Happy suggested. 'Besides, this ain't a healthy place to be foolin' around—not after what's happened.'

Gentleman Jim started. He realized that he had been standing for some time, lost in thought. Happy had waited with the fidelity of a dog.

'Go on, Happy,' he said. 'I'll be along pretty soon.'

Happy hesitated, made as if to protest, then vanished in the gloom. Gentleman Jim followed slowly. He had reached the front porch when he became aware of a shadowy figure lurking there, and he tensed. Then he saw that it was Maita.

She came toward him and in the half-light her eyes were wide with anxiety.

'You're back!' she whispered. 'I had to know! I heard what you were doing! But there was no shooting?'

'No,' he said. 'No shooting. No trouble, to speak of.'

She drew a sighing breath.

'You're a strange man,' she whispered.

'A strange one, indeed,' Gentleman Jim agreed. 'Tonight I was a gambler.'

'But in a good cause,' she said, and now her eyes seemed to reflect the stars. 'Oh, the word is all over town—how you might have killed him, but spared him instead! You—you are very good.'

She turned then and was gone quickly, almost shyly. But her praise had been sweet, and heady like wine.

## CHAPTER EIGHTEEN

# BIG NOSE

There was a changed attitude in town the next morning. Gentleman Jim became aware of it at the breakfast table, in the way John Gilson looked at him. These people had liked him before, had come to respect and to hold him in some esteem. But his exploits of the evening had added to his stature.

The big saloon was locked tight today, as he had instructed. No one among the bartenders who had worked there for Deal Hathaway had disputed his right to give those orders, whatever might be their personal loyalties.

His talk—lecture seemed the wrong
166

word—went well enough. If they had expected anything new or big, he didn't give it to them. How could a man point a course, when he didn't know where he was going himself?

As soon as he could get away, he moved off by himself, back toward the coulee. The trees and brush, the cool stream winding out from the hills, looked inviting. He must have a chance to think, though what good that would do he couldn't figure. Everybody was busy now—the women preparing a big picnic dinner for everybody, the men standing around and waiting expectantly for a chance to eat it. It would be a little while before it was ready. He'd have to be there, then. That was expected of him—

'Looks like you're puttin' it over, Jim.'

He spun about, startled. Then he saw him, standing in the shadow of the hangman's tree. Big Nose Sullivan.

For a moment the shock left him speechless. He had supposed that Big Nose was a long way from here, helping to care for and keep watch over Timothy Meader and John Widdicombe. On second thought, he realized that he was slipping badly, not to have foreseen that either Big Nose or the Weasel would be coming right along at his heels, to keep watch on what he did. There was nothing trusting about those two.

'You gave me a scare, Big Nose,' he said.

'I didn't know you were here.'

'Well, I've been keepin' pretty well out of sight, since I hit town last night,' Big Nose explained. 'I'd have liked to get close enough to hear your spiel just now, just to see how you could hand it out, but I couldn't quite manage that. Looks like you were putting it over big as usual, though. Folks is suckers, ain't they?'

'I guess maybe they are,' Gentleman Jim agreed. 'Most of us are—whether we know it or not. But aren't you taking a long chance, leaving the Weasel with Meader?'

'Not so long a one as it would have been to send him here,' Big Nose pointed out. 'I figured that you and Happy might be needin' some help, and the idea was that I was to come along and be ready to lend a hand when needed. From all I can pick up, you've been doing a fine piece of work, Jim. You're a better actor than I figured—and I knew you were good.'

Gentleman Jim brushed that aside.

'How is Meader's leg getting along?'

'Doing all right,' Big Nose said impatiently. 'But he ain't nothin' for us to worry about. From what I hear, you've got things about ready for the clean-up. Guess I didn't get here none too soon, eh?'

Here was danger—trouble which he should have foreseen. Only it had arrived sooner than he had expected.

168

'There's no rush, so far as that's concerned,' Gentleman Jim said carelessly.

Big Nose eyed him sharply.

'Don't crowd your luck too far, Jim,' he warned. 'You've been havin' a run of it to make a jackrabbit jealous, from what I hear. You always used to say to make a fast clean-up and get out while the going was good. And there's another thing. After what you did last night—well, you'd ought to know what I mean. You should have killed that Deal Hathaway while you had the chance. That hombre's poison. And he'll strike, first chance he gets.'

*This is it!* Gentleman Jim thought grimly. *You can't keep on riding two horses heading opposite ways!* On the one side was what he had come after, comparative safety—the always doubtful safety of a hunted man. On the other side—

On the other side was a girl, and that intangible thing called honour. A girl who would hate him when she knew, in any case. An honour which no one would ever sense or attribute to him. And, alongside the two, certain disaster. It could be no other way—

'Do I have to throw a rope over that limb up there and get it around your neck to attract your attention?' He became aware that Big Nose was talking, a peevish note in his voice. 'What's eatin' you, Jim? I know you've been busy—that you've done the

169

best job of your career, and I reckon you've got plenty on your mind. But my notion was that we'd ought to talk this over, and there won't be much chance.'

'I'll have to be getting back to the dinner, or they'll be coming after me,' Gentleman Jim said hurriedly. 'After it's over, I'll try and stroll out here and maybe we can have a better chance then.'

'All right,' Big Nose agreed. 'You said you'd get their confidence, and that after that you could manage the rest of it all right. Seems like you've done both. Though I thought you was crazy, when I heard how they came and wanted you to take that money, and you shied away from it like a boogery cayuse!'

Gentleman Jim's face was stony. But Big Nose was in a high good humour.

'Crazy like a fox, wasn't you?' he added. 'Tellin' them to turn it over to Hathaway and put it in *his* safe for safe keepin'! And now it's in *your* safe, since you own everything that Deal Hathaway had, includin' the safe!'

# CHAPTER NINETEEN

## HAPPY DISAPPEARS

*His* safe! He hadn't thought of it in that light before, but in a sense it was true. Everything that he had hoped to do, when first coming to Hangman's Coulee, was working out as he had planned, and better than he had expected. All that he needed to do was take the money and get out between two days.

It would be simple. He would be what he had been before, a thief—wanted by the law. Gentleman Jim Thornton, with the biggest, neatest job of his career behind him. And he would leave disillusionment and broken hearts. Though that would not be all that was left. His own would be included.

That was one solution. No matter what he did now, it would be wrong. Hangman's Coulee! They had named it better than they knew.

There was one small matter which he had temporarily forgotten. He saw Nobel Cutting's red head among a group of those who were preparing the dinner, and one look at him was proof enough that Gentleman Jim's promise to restore his money to him had not reached back to Cutting's ears. He was the picture now of a penitent man, anxious to make up for his own shortcomings, and not quite sure how to do it.

Cutting was a big man who had married young. He still had the look of an overgrown boy, but today his face was sober amid the general air of festivity, and he remained close to his wife, who could walk under his outstretched arm. There was a dog-like devotion in his face, and his eyes followed her everywhere.

She, at least, possessed the spirit of the pioneers, to spit in the eye of danger and laugh in the face of trouble. Despite the disaster which had overtaken them, she was busily helping with the dinner, laughing and joking. Now she tossed her head in answer to some question.

'We'll make out,' she declared with a confidence which she probably did not feel. 'I've always observed that people generally manage to live till they die—and we only die once. So what's there to worry about?'

'*I'd* be worried, if 'twas me,' another lady returned, mopping perspiring face. 'Not, I s'pose, that worryin' does any good, only it'd fret me not to be able—oh, here's the Professor. You workin' up an appetite, eh, Professor?'

'I'm starved,' Gentleman Jim agreed

promptly, though his thoughts had been far from food. 'How could a man walk in the midst of such a succulent display without his mouth watering?' Offhandedly, as if it was an afterthought, he reached into a pocket, pulled out a roll of bills and tendered them in the astonished face of Cutting. 'Oh, by the way, these are yours,' he said. 'With the compliments of Deal Hathaway. He suffered a change of heart, after he'd had time to think it over.'

'M-mine?' Cutting stared, not quite believing. Then, as he understood, light came into his face like sunrise over a hill. 'You—you mean, Professor—that you got it back for me—'

It was his wife who burst suddenly into tears. Where her woebegone husband had now taken on the aspects of an exuberant puppy, she sank down and put her apron over her face, sobbing. Cutting blinked in sheer astonishment, then touched her shoulder tentatively.

'W-what's the trouble, Honeycake?' he demanded. 'It's all fine now. We're going to make out big—'

'Of course we are,' she agreed, jumping up, and before Gentleman Jim suspected her purpose, she had leaned forward to kiss him on the cheek. Her black eyes were sparkling through her tears, but her voice was still muffled.

'I've heard before about entertaining angels unawares,' she said. 'Though this time we should have known—'

Sam Staves came up at that moment, to Gentleman Jim's relief, and his big voice boomed out across the grounds.

'Everything's ready, folks,' he called. 'Here's good food just waiting to be eaten; let's do our duty by it, so the ladies won't feel disappointed!'

Gentleman Jim was silent a moment. An angel, she had called him, at least by implication. Nothing else had moved him as that, and her kiss, had done. Now he knew, with sudden clearness, what he was going to do. Too many were involved in this besides himself. There could be only one outcome, but what else had she said? That we die but once.

He saw the sheriff, one of a group about another table, and on impulse, moved in that direction.

He noted, with some surprise, that Happy was actually laughing. Happy seemed to have put aside his worries for the moment. He was seated on the grass alongside Minerva Staves, a heaping plate in his lap, a chicken leg in his hand. Strange behaviour for Happy, but there was almost a schoolgirl colour in Minerva's cheeks today.

Maita had reserved a place beside her for Jim, and he took it gratefully, accepting the plate which she filled and passed to him. His foster-parents were a part of the circle, and she was looking after their wants with a careful regard.

The funeral service was to be held in the big tent, once dinner was out of the way. Since Ten-Spot had declared himself on the Professor's side, it was counted as only fitting that everyone who felt the same way should attend the ceremony. Certainly Ten-Spot's end was to be different than it would have been had the bullet overtaken him a few days earlier.

It was as the service was about to begin that Gentleman Jim discovered that Happy was absent. He had been well fed and apparently happy, but no one had seen him for the last half-hour, and a quick check failed to find him.

'And he seemed to be enjoyin' himself, too,' Minerva said, puzzled. 'I can't think where he could have gone to. He was supposed to stay with me. Just wait till I see him again!'

That sounded suspiciously like a Staves talking, but Gentleman Jim had a sudden uneasy suspicion. For the moment, however, it was impossible to do anything about it. He had to say a few words over Ten-Spot.

'I can play for you, if you wish,' Maita volunteered, and Gentleman Jim accepted.

But now his doubts were increasing, as he remembered various details of Happy's recent behaviour. Since it was Happy who was concerned, they could be serious.

In that guess he was correct. Happy had reached the breaking point. It had started the evening before when he had gone along with Gentleman Jim to the Cattleman's. The big saloon, with its row on row of bottles, had filled him with nostalgia. The nearness of liquor had been a heady temptation. Only the tenseness of the situation and the fact that he had a job to do had enabled Happy to keep his mind on the latter.

When the game was ended and there had been no shedding of blood, the let-down had been doubly hard. He had been keyed to use his own gun, to fight his way through as big a bar-room brawl as he had ever known, and nothing much had happened.

Temptation was in his way, as they left the saloon. Someone had left a bottle on a table. It was easy enough to reach out and slip it under the skirts of his coat with no one noticing. Even as he did so, Happy had assured himself that he wouldn't actually take a drink—not while they remained in Hangman's Coulee, with the constant threat of exposure hanging over them.

But one thing was certain. This sort of thing couldn't go on, not much longer.

When the break came, he'd need something to help tide him over it, and by that time it could no longer matter if he washed out his throat with a drop or so of whisky.

He cached the bottle for the night, pleased to have it in reserve. But daylight had brought an appalling discovery. The bottle had been more than half-emptied by its original purchaser. In his haste the night before, the need to keep Gentleman Jim from observing what he was about, he had failed to notice its state of depletion.

Discovery filled Happy with a quivering rage, the futile wrath of twanging nerves. But as the day wore on this was replaced with a new notion. Since there was only a little in the bottle in any case, why shouldn't he drink it? Just one good drink. That much couldn't hurt him.

One drink, of course, had a habit of leading to another, as Happy had long since learned. But this time, he wouldn't have a chance to get an extra drink, so it would be all right.

There were, after all, two drinks in the bottle. The first one filled him with a pleasant sense of well-being which yielded to an overpowering sense of thirst. Restlessness came upon him. As soon as the morning lecture was out of the way, he got rid of the bottle and what remained in it. And again, for a little while, well-being descended upon him.

That, in turn, yielded again to the overwhelming desire for another drink. By the time dinner was out of the way, Happy knew that he had to have it. Though it should lead him straight to a noose under the hanging tree itself, he was powerless now to stop. He'd slip away, get a bottle and be back before anyone had missed him. Beyond that, he did not think. When ugly notions tried to obtrude, he deliberately shoved them aside. A drink, now, was vital as breath itself.

It would be simple. He'd go to the big saloon and make a brief tour of inspection. Since the bartenders knew him for the Professor's right-hand man, they wouldn't see anything strange in it. It would be easy.

There was just one contingency that he had failed to take into consideration. He already had a bottle in his hand and was holding it, debating whether to open it now or later, when a familiar voice spoke at his shoulder.

'Well, well! It looks as if here's one man who's a judge of good whisky, at least!'

Happy turned, startled. Deal Hathaway was smiling down at him. Happy tried to back away, but something in the gambler's eyes seemed to mesmerize him. Or, more accurately, it might have been what Hathaway held in his hand—a glass of whisky, freshly poured. He still had the open bottle in his other hand, and now he tendered the glass.

'Here,' he invited. 'Let's have a drink and talk this over!'

## CHAPTER TWENTY

# THE NECKTIE PARTY

A flurry of gunshots climaxed the lowering of Ten-Spot Lolo into the earth. A more appropriate dirge, perhaps, than the hymn which a group of the ladies had just sung over him, save that the shots came from some distance way, followed by what might have been wild rebel yells. Only there was a quality to these sounds more savage than the cries of fighting men. In them was all the deep-throated savagery of a wolf pack at the kill. This was the voice of a mob.

The turmoil was continuing, though the firing had stopped. All of it came now from the vicinity of the big tree, not very far away.

Most of the audience who had attended the morning lecture were at the funeral, but enough people had been left in the town to make up a rival crowd. Now, raising startled heads, the mourners listened briefly. Very little time was required for the majority of the men present to interpret those other sounds and to decide that the tree was now the point of chief interest on the local scene. They stampeded as though some sort of a plague had begun to pour up from the hole where Ten-Spot had been lowered.

Gentleman Jim listened momentarily, then he too was running. The crowd was ten deep as he neared the big tree, and at first all that he could see was that a rope was over the limb of it. Then, as he elbowed closer, he saw that half a dozen men had hold of the other end of the rope and were preparing to pull.

Standing beneath the tree, blood smearing his face, held erect by two other men, was Big Nose Sullivan. The hempen necktie was about his throat, already chokingly tight.

'Heave away!' a red-whiskered man shouted. 'Let's see how he can dance a jig on air! Be good practice for the dancin' he'll do in hell tonight!'

Gentleman Jim hesitated momentarily. Here was an outlaw, who deserved what he was getting, a man who had come here at the wrong moment, who could be a menace. A man who would be relentless and remorseless. He had only to stand back, and again luck would play into his hands—

Then, with a gasping cry, Gentleman Jim

was fighting his way closer. He was like a madman, and they gave way before him. But as the two men beside the outlaw shrank back, Big Nose sagged in the noose. The man who appeared to be the ringleader spat. There was a derisive curl to his flaming beard, a bantering sort of savage amusement in deep-set eyes.

'Don't get het up, Professor,' he suggested. 'This is Big Nose Sullivan—an' everybody knows who he is! We caught him snoopin' around out here—so we're going to give him all the hangin' around he wants!'

Gentleman Jim was beside Big Nose now, one arm about him, supporting his sagging figure, but the outlaw boss was a dead weight in his grasp. Jim faced them angrily, a sickness in the pit of his stomach. It might so easily have been himself in this spot, and it still might be!

'Outlaw he may be,' he said. 'And maybe in need of hanging! But any man has a right to a fair trial! You've a sheriff in this town. Let him handle it. Don't stain your hands with the blood of any man!'

Again the ringleader spat, grinning crookedly.

'Them's nice words, Professor, and mebby they'd apply—ordinary,' he agreed. 'Only, if you'll look, you'll see that hangin' ain't goin' to make much diff'rence to him, anyhow! He stopped two or three bullets 'fore we got to him. Deader'n a mackerel. Though he did all right for himself, shootin' back! Look!'

He lifted one brawny arm, down which blood was running, and laughed at the wound.

'My luck,' he said. 'And his run out! And since he sure needed hangin', we're stringin' him up—as an example and a warnin' to any others of his gang as to what they'll get if *they* come sneakin' around here! So stand aside, Professor. I reckon you mean well, but it's a waste of breath in this case. And we're hoistin' him. Which is likely the closest to heaven he'll ever get!'

## CHAPTER TWENTY-ONE

# SHOWDOWN

Clouds were building in the west, spreading with a slow but ominous patience. A low wind moved through the branches like a dirge—perhaps for the soul of him who had swung beneath the tree until a scant half-hour before.

Gentleman Jim turned soberly toward the big meeting tent. The hanging of Big Nose had brought a flurry of excitement, but now it was over with. The more sober-minded might deplore the way in which it had happened, but it was nothing new for Hangman's Coulee, and for the most part they had forgotten it. There would be no lessening of the evening crowd on account of it.

There was still no sign of Happy. Gentleman Jim hoped that he had taken warning and gotten out of town. He felt a responsibility for Happy, doubled since the grim climax of the afternoon. Yet he had to speak tonight, in one final lecture, come what might. After that it would be out of his hands. All that he knew was that this was his choice. Better a swift finish than to be hunted down the years, finally to end in a noose. Those years would be worse than empty, futile, filled with frustration.

Maita was at the organ again. She smiled at him in a way which made him catch his breath, and then began to play. His eyes searched the audience. The McGilroys were not here this evening. And that, perhaps, was just as well.

'A man was hanged this afternoon,' Gentleman Jim said. 'Some of you were shocked, others were even smugly complacent that it was a good deed well done. So far as the welfare of the community is concerned, that is probably true. There's no doubt that he deserved what he got. But if we were to get what we deserve—would any of us be any better off?

'I'm not going to lecture tonight. I'm going to talk to you—more honestly than I've ever done before. And to begin with, Big Nose Sullivan was a man whom I both admired and hated. And, in a manner of speaking, he was also my friend.'

He saw the startled looks on the faces below him, went on levelly.

'I'm well aware that I've been a strange sort of a professor since I came here. That I've done a lot of things which have puzzled and shocked some of you. What I'm going to say to you now will even more so. For my own part, I have only one request to make. That is that you will suspend judgment and listen to what I have to say, first. I'm going to talk about myself.'

'I've only one defence. I could go away from here without saying anything, as I had once intended to do. Maybe some of you will think I'm a fool not to do so. Maybe I am. But there's that course—or this one. And, strangely enough, I prefer this one.'

His smile, for a moment, broke gravely through.

'The other evening I told you something of what my life had been. But I told only a part. There were two reasons then why I made the confession that I did. One was because my foster-father had stood up and

184

called me a liar and a scoundrel—which I knew to be the truth. The fact that what he said was true had enough effect on me that I had to admit it.'

They were listening now with tense interest. There had been drama in his confession before, but they sensed that this would be more so.

'I suppose I might tell you that I've had a change of heart since coming to your town. In a way, that would be true. But it's more than that. I've talked to you about things that I didn't know I believed in—and I find that I do! I didn't intend to do anything like this when I came here. In fact, I had entirely different plans in mind when I headed this way.'

He caught Maita's intent look on him, and for a moment his voice faltered. Then he went on, like a man wading a swift, cold stream.

'Please understand that I'm not making any excuses for myself. It's only that I've come up against some square and decent people—including my foster-parents—for the first time in a good many years. They are going to be shocked and hurt, but maybe, in a small way, they can be proud of me, too—that I've got at least a little manhood in me. The other way they would be even more shocked and hurt. I've worked myself into a corner, and I'm not being

185

noble. There're only two ways out—to walk out, or to drop through a trap door.'

Again he was silent for a moment, and silence held the audience. They could sense how hard it was for him to say these words. As though each one had been the deep-bedded quill of a porcupine, hooked on the end, which he must jerk out of the quivering flesh.

'You hanged Big Nose Sullivan today. And I hated Big Nose for what he was—a cruel and brutal man, a killer. I hated him because he had me more or less in his power. It was partly, maybe largely, because of him, that I came here in the first place.'

He was aware that Maita's eyes were on him, but now he dared not look toward her.

'My real purpose in coming here was not to lecture to you or to talk about civic improvement. That was to be only a blind. What I intended was to steal that hundred thousand dollars which you of this community have raised for the railroad, to ensure that it should pass through this town. Big Nose Sullivan was to help me do it.'

Shock and incredulity were written large on their faces now. Giving them no chance to recover, he went on.

'In my day I have played a great many roles, so that I have become something of an actor. I was sure that I could play the role of a professor and do it so well that you would all be fooled. And that, after gaining your confidence in such a manner, I would have little difficulty in getting hold of that money, and decamping between two days. Let me repeat that I'm not telling you this for an excuse. I deserve to wear a rope about my neck as much as Big Nose Sullivan did, and once I'm finished, if you want it that way, I'll be right here.

'What I didn't count on was the friends I'd make—square shooters, decent folks. Or finding my foster-parents here, and the effect it would have on them if I went through with my original programme. I'm not offering this as an excuse. I'm just telling you why I'm saying all this. I couldn't hurt them, and double-cross the friends I'd made here. Not any more than I could help.'

Still no one moved to interrupt, and he went on.

'One thing that affected me, I think, was the clothes that I'm wearing. The garments of a real man. I've no right to them, but I'm wearing them.

'They belong to the real Timothy Meader—who will probably be among you, in good health, some day soon. I constrained him to let me borrow them, against his will.

'I hadn't been here long before I became scared of the situation I'd got into.

187

Frightened on account of how what I was going to do would affect others. Particularly I was worried about my companion, who has played the organ. You've heard of him—not John Widdicombe, but Happy Brant. Happy is a good-hearted, harmless sort of man who, like myself, drifted downward until he was consorting with outlaws. But Happy is a man who, of his own accord, has never committed a crime or done a mean thing that I have ever known of. I hope that you'll give him a chance.'

He looked out at them for a long moment, and saw the mingled emotions on many faces. Shock, incredulity, bewilderment.

'I got the idea of taking Professor Meader's place so that I could cheat you. I fell into the trap of my own setting. But I think that he, the real Professor, will be coming along in a few days. When he does come, I want you to listen to what he has to say to you, without discounting it because of what I've said and done. He's all that I'm not.'

'Then who the blazes are you?' someone demanded, from a row near the rear.

*Here it is*, he thought. Though most of them must have guessed already. He looked back, trying to pick out who had spoken, and tensed as his eyes fixed on another

188

man, seated quietly near the edge of the tent. A man who was listening with an appearance of quiet interest, even of enjoyment.

For a moment, the surprise of the discovery held him silent. Somehow, this was the last thing that he had been prepared for—that Timothy Meader himself should be here, in this audience. His wound, of course, had been a minor thing, and was probably about healed now.

At least, the real Professor had not denounced him at the start, nor shouted for the sheriff. Timothy Meader, he was more than ever convinced, was quite a man.

There was comfort in the knowledge that he was here. He could keep these folks from losing all faith in everything decent, following his own downfall. There was a commotion near the rear of the tent now, but he paid it no attention as he answered.

'That's a fair question, and I'll give you a straight answer. I've been known for—'

'There he is, Sheriff! That's him—the outlaw known as Gentleman Jim Thornton!'

## CHAPTER TWENTY-TWO

# HATHAWAY'S GAMBLE

The exclamation, drowning out his own words, was shouted from where a small group of men had thrust inside the tent. They were led by Deal Hathaway.

The light was fading fast, and inside the big tent it was almost murky. In the gloom it would be easy to stir up confusion, but it would not be hard to make a getaway. He'd done so, under somewhat similar circumstances, more than once. But tonight the thought held no appeal.

He would make, Gentleman Jim supposed, one last short journey—across to Hangman's Tree, where Big Nose Sullivan had died so short a time before. Such a journey seemed inevitable, unless the sheriff intervened. He was an outlaw. But in any case, as he had already decided, it would be better that way. Nora, who had cherished hopes for him, could at least think of him kindly. And Nora represented many, whose opinion had suddenly become of great value.

He understood now what had happened to Happy. Happy had succumbed to the desire for one drink—and Deal Hathaway had plied him with more. Until, with his tongue loosened, Happy had babbled into the gambler's ear all that he wanted to know. Now, armed with this knowledge, Hathaway had come here, confident of discrediting him and the whole movement into whose leadership he had been thrust, of taking back his saloons and place of leadership in the town in the same act.

Hathaway stirred impatiently as the crowd turned to look at him, and from him to where the Professor stood. If he had hoped to create a sensation, he was disappointed. No one seemed particularly surprised. Even the sheriff stood phlegmatically. Hathaway seized his arm and shook him.

'Don't you understand?' he repeated. 'He's Gentleman Jim Thornton—the outlaw! And he's got that hundred thousand dollars that was raised for the railroad, in his safe, right now—unless he's already gotten away with it!'

The sheriff twisted his arm loose and grunted.

'If it's in the safe, then it ought to be safe,' he pointed out reasonably.

'What the devil's the matter with you?' Hathaway's voice rose angrily. 'Can't you understand what I said—that he's Gentleman Jim Thornton—'

'Yeah,' Hoffman nodded. 'He's just been

tellin' us all about himself. Course, I've known who he was, ever since the first day he hit town.'

'You've known it—' Hathaway eyed the sheriff in an amazement shared now by Gentleman Jim himself. 'You've known he was an outlaw,' he repeated, his voice rising, 'and you let him masquerade as a professor of some sort, and haven't done a damned thing about it! What sort of a sheriff are you, anyhow?'

Hoffman rubbed his chin reflectively.

'Kind of a poor one, I guess,' he conceded. 'Considerin' that you've run a pretty rank layout here for quite a spell, Deal, and I ain't done nothin' about it—chiefly because folks seemed to want it that way, and what folks want they generally get. Likewise, I didn't have no direct evidence to act on, no matter how much I might have suspicioned you of runnin' a crooked set of games—'

'Are we talking about me, or about a known outlaw?' Hathaway interrupted savagely. 'Of course you've had nothing against me. But you say you knew all along who he was, and that he's a wanted man—'

'Yeah,' the sheriff agreed, while the attention of everyone now centred on these two. 'But he was here as a lecturin' sort of professor, to entertain and instruct—and I had two things in mind. First off, I didn't want to get everybody that amounted to anything, down on my neck, by arrestin' their imported word-slinger. I knew who he was, but I couldn't make out, right then, to prove it. And a professor rates near as high in folks' opinions as a sky pilot. Second, I figured if I give him rope enough, he'd catch himself up in it and prove it on himself—'

'Which he's done,' Hathaway cut in. 'You've got the proof of that now. So why don't you arrest him?'

The sheriff shook his head stubbornly.

'I just been listenin' to him admit who he was, and what he come here for,' he said mildly. 'To him tellin' how he'd had a change of heart—'

'And do you believe that? It's just a trick to cover up while he gets away—'

'Funny sort of trick, then, when he could've done it a whole lot easier by keepin' his mouth shut. Fact is, more I hear him talk, the better I like him. I figgered it was all a trick at first, but I changed my mind. I been watchin' him to see what he'd do. And I sure ain't got no cause for complaint on what he's been doing since he hit this town. Not any.'

'No?' Deal Hathaway's voice was rough with sarcasm. 'Maybe you don't know that he came to town to steal that hundred thousand that was raised for the railroad—'

'Sure I do. You mentioned it first off. But

193

he'd explained all about that himself—
before you come bustin' in here.'

'He explained—' Hathaway's jaw sagged.
Then he recovered angrily.

'But if you know he came to steal—hell's
fire, Sheriff, what does it take to make you
fill your office? His confederates are in town
now. We caught Big Nose, but the Weasel
is sure to be around. They'll be getting away
with the money while you gabble. I tell you
it's just a stall to give them time—'

The sheriff shook his head.

'I doubt it,' he denied. 'I ain't so big a
fool but I can see *why* he's had more'n a
bellyful of the old life. But as to that money
that's worryin' you so much, why the
Professor—or Thornton, or whatever you
want to call him—he turned that money
over to me for safe keepin', hours ago. I got
some deputies watchin' it now. When he
done that, I had my answer for sure, and I
knew that *I* didn't want him.'

Hathaway was fighting for control.
Readjusting his notions to what he had just
heard was not easy. There was no doubt but
what he was as surprised as Gentleman Jim
himself had been that he should have acted
in such a manner. Such a course, to a man
like Deal Hathaway, was incomprehensible.
Just as it would have been to Gentleman
Jim a scant week earlier.

But Hathaway was figuring it out, and,

194

though he might never understand the impelling reasons back of it, that was a minor point. He could feel how the wind was blowing. Worse than that, he could see defeat where a moment before he had envisioned victory. Somehow, Gentleman Jim had won this crowd, and they were behind him—as much so now, encouraged by the sheriff's stand, as they had been before.

Which spelled showdown. Not the sort he had counted on a few minutes before, but even more decisive. Tonight he had everything to gain and nothing to lose. And he had come here prepared for any eventuality.

'So you refuse to take action, to arrest him?' Hathaway demanded, tight-lipped. 'As an officer of the law, you won't do a thing?'

'Depends on what you call action, I guess,' the sheriff retorted.

Hathaway's voice took on a new note of command.

'Then it's up to the honest citizens of this town to take action themselves, the same as we've had to do to clean up in the past! Come on, boys! Let's string this outlaw up where his partner was this afternoon!'

Even as he spoke a gun was in his hand and he was plunging ahead. For a moment Gentleman Jim, himself a little dazed with the turn of events, was in doubt as to just what he might have in mind. Whether Hathaway still believed that, led by himself and a handful of his followers, the old mob instinct could be roused as before, or not. The light was uncertain, all to the advantage of such a plan as Hathaway might have in mind. And he was wringing all the benefit possible from it.

Gentleman Jim had been listening to this latest exchange as though he had been a detached spectator, having no particular interest in the outcome. It seemed harder to believe than anything which had gone before, the things which the sheriff had said—or that they could be about him. Certainly he had expected no such reaction.

But while one part of his mind was remote, he was keyed physically to a high pitch. Here, though in slightly different form than he had expected, was the test. And now it was involving others than himself.

He heard Maita's scream, choked short off, and spun about to see her struggling in the arms of Deal Hathaway. The next moment she had been jerked off the platform and the two of them were gone in the gloom, out past the fringes of the tent.

Taking advantage of the night and the confusion, Hathaway had darted back and around to grab Maita before anyone

196

suspected what he was up to. His shout had been a bluff—a gesture to confuse, and it had accomplished its purpose. Under cover of that he had a desperate plan, one which might work due to its sheer boldness.

With Maita for a hostage he might dictate terms as his own followers rallied, and get away with it. If he failed, he'd take her with him. And that was understandable, for a man who thought as did Deal Hathaway. He had dwelt on the fringes of respectability, but that was an alien place to him. With him it was all or nothing, and even the woman he professed to love was, as she had always been, only a pawn in the game.

Several of his own men had followed him here, and they were helping now—shouting, creating confusion, some of them deliberately leading off in a wrong direction. As he burst out of the tent, Gentleman Jim had a glimpse of Hathaway, swinging onto a saddled horse, still carrying Maita like a helpless bundle in his arms. But most of the crowd, as they poured out from the tent, was being beguiled into following the other way.

That was what Deal Hathaway wanted—just a little time. Which he wasn't going to have. There was another horse handy, left by some cowboy who had come to the lecture. Gentleman Jim knew, within

197

an instant after he had hit the saddle, that this cayuse could run.

All that he had to do was let it have its head. The horse seemed to feel as he did—that the important thing was to get to Maita as quickly as possible. It was gaining on the doubly burdened cayuse ahead, and Deal Hathaway had to change his plans again.

Whatever he had counted on, here was nemesis on his trail. But luck hadn't deserted him, not yet. There was a blur of white at the edge of the road, up ahead. This swiftly resolved itself into the canvas top of a wagon as they swept toward it. An equipage much like the covered wagon in which the Professor had travelled the country, and the one in which Gentleman Jim had come to this town. This wagon, as luck would have it, was standing, with a team hitched to it.

Hathaway was having his hands full. Maita was not a docile captive. She kicked and clawed and scratched like a fury, and Hathaway, angered, hit her with a cold deliberation, a blow which rocked her head back and then left her limp in his grasp, knocked cold. Gentleman Jim saw it and choked, and urged his horse to greater speed.

But the gambler, like himself, was schooled to cool thinking in emergencies.

He headed for the wagon, and lost scarcely a moment in making the transfer when he reached it, jumping across the wheel and onto it, still with Maita in his arms, allowing his cayuse to run. Then, dumping her on the floor behind the seat, he snatched up the reins, which had been wrapped around the brake bar, and urged the startled team to a trot, and from that to a lumbering gallop.

The delay of this operation had been costly, for Gentleman Jim had halved the distance between them. But now they were out of town, heading onto a road which was new to Gentleman Jim. Now they were far enough out that, with more gunfire and confusion behind them, a few extra shots would attract no particular attention, add nothing to the hazard for the gambler.

He was counting the odds now as coolly as he played a game of cards, with none of the jumpy nerves which had affected him the night before. The light was poor, only a thin moon and high remote stars blinking through a wrack of broken clouds, but good enough at that distance. Deal Hathaway swung part way round on the wagon seat, his gun lifting. Flame lanced out from it like the thin and wicked tongue of a rattlesnake.

Now the distance between them had almost been wiped out—enough so that, even at an uncertain running target, a gunman like Hathaway could not miss. Gentleman Jim heard the sighing grunt of his straining cayuse, felt it falter in its stride and knew that it was going down under him. And if he went down with the horse now, it would be to defeat.

There was a gallant strain in this horse, a will to victory which even death could not spoil. Heritage of the great blood of Spanish ancestors, of wild horses battling heavy odds to exist. It made one last effort, and that brought it even with the rear of the wagon. As it collapsed, Gentleman Jim flung himself off, and he knew that he had to equal the last spurt of the horse. He was falling short, missing—and then his fingers found the wooden end gate of the wagon box, brushed the loose canvas aside and held fast.

His feet struck the ground, running, the wagon jerking him along. For a moment he clung there, then lifted himself and climbed inside.

There was one similarity of this wagon to the Professor's, in that both were canvas-topped. There the resemblance ended, and his nose told him sharply what sort this was. A sheep herder's wagon, living quarters on the range. And odours of sheep and camp were impregnated in it. But the herder had driven a good team.

They were running at a headlong gallop,

200

and for the moment Deal Hathaway had been too much occupied to pay attention to them. He spun about on the seat now, alarmed more by instinct than sound or sight, for the bumping wagon was making noise enough and the canvas cut off even the uncertain starlight. But he saw the shadowy figure of Gentleman Jim, halfway up the length of the wagon, and swung his gun and fired again at point blank range—and missed.

The hammer clicked then on empty shells, and Gentleman Jim, all but stumbling over the prone figure of Maita in the bottom of the wagon, closed with him. The wagon seat was knocked loose and teetered for a precarious moment at the side of the jouncing box, then went off and was out of the way.

They were locked together, straining desperately, man to man at last. A section of the canvas ripped back and away, giving them the benefit of the half-light, and dismay came with it. Hathaway had wrapped the lines about the brake lever, leaving the horses to their own devices, and now, terror-driven, they were running away.

But that was not the worst. This was a mountain dug-road where they raced, and off at the side, scant inches beyond the outer wheels, was only reaching darkness—with a vast void of emptiness below.

## CHAPTER TWENTY-THREE

# THE DEVIL'S BOWL

All of this was new country to him, but Gentleman Jim knew where they were. He had heard of this particular stretch of road, one little used but given the graphically descriptive name of the Devil's Bowl. It was the bowl down below now, around the side of which, for nearly a mile, the road circled. Report had it as a narrow and precarious trail, with dizzy depths at its side. The look of it, even in the night, seemed to confirm the worse tales which were told. If one wheel went off at the edge, nothing could save them.

Whatever had been the plan or the mood of Deal Hathaway a few minutes before, it had been displaced now by the cold recklessness of the gambler who stakes everything on one turn of the cards. More than once it had seemed to Hathaway that this man was his personal nemesis, but more than once in the contest he had been certain that he held victory in his grasp. And now it was a primitive struggle, man to man, and both of them knew that it was final. This would end it, one way or the other—and for one of them.

In that mood, there was only savage exultation in Deal Hathaway. He was a powerful man, and in the first few moments there had been certainty in him that he would win. Now, straining desperately, doubt crept into his mind, but it was a spur to goad him on. There was another way to win—a sure one and quick. In this mood he did not hesitate.

He took advantage of a lurch of the wagon to break away and step back, and the next instant he had stooped and raised up again with the still inert figure of Maita in his arms. Balancing against the sway of the wagon, he held her, poised, and his laugh had a touch of madness in it.

'Keep back, Thornton,' he warned, 'or I'll throw her over—I warned you at the start that I intended to have her! If I don't, no man does—least of all you!'

He was breathing hard, and the wagon was still jerking along at a headlong pace, somehow staying on the narrow ribbon of road. Hathaway's voice rapped incisively.

'But it has to be her or you out of here now! This is it—*Professor*! If you love her—jump! Otherwise, it's her.'

Coldness was like a knotted fist in Gentleman Jim's stomach. He knew that the gambler meant exactly as he threatened. At each new deal of this game he had grown more recklessly determined on his course.

The goading prick of conviction that he was wrong from the start had only hardened his resolution.

Now, if Gentleman Jim took that wild leap outward to destruction, it would save the life of the woman he loved. Also, it would deliver her into the power of this ruthless man, just as it must do with the town also. Only one man had ever seriously threatened Deal Hathaway, and he was making his last big gamble on that.

Here was another of the intangibles— forces which had pushed Gentleman Jim Thornton to make his choice and to act the way he had. Rivalry with this man who, working within the cloak of the law, had been far beyond it. And who, by those acts, had driven Gentleman Jim Thornton to the side of the law.

If he didn't jump now—then Hathaway would sacrifice her. Since, in his own twisted way, he loved her, he would plan to go with her in that final plunge. It was the sort of dramatic act to appeal to the gambling heart of the man, an all or nothing gesture.

The pinch was that he had the whip hand now. It was take him at his terms or see him do it. Poised as he was at the edge of the wagon box, where the canvas had torn away, it would be impossible for Gentleman Jim to close the distance between them in time to prevent him from carrying out his threat.

'No,' Gentleman Jim choked. 'Don't do it—'

Incredibly, there was help at hand—a shapeless form that rose up behind Deal Hathaway, shoving at him, clutching at the burden he held in his arms as he turned. The surprise of it staggered Hathaway, and then he was crying out, in a mixture of wild anger and pleading.

'Don't be a fool, Weasel—help me, man! We're both on the same side—'

The Weasel, a grotesque figure, only grunted. The struggle became more fierce, and as the wagon lurched again, Hathaway lost his balance. He tried desperately to regain it, while the Weasel tore Maita away from him.

For a moment Hathaway teetered, then, like an actor bowing offstage, took one step backward and was gone.

Incredulity and confusion were in Gentleman Jim, but there was a job of desperate urgency, and he leaped to grab the reins off the brake lever, throwing his weight against them as he shouted at the running horses. With one foot he kicked the brake on, hard.

For a minute longer it was a race with death, there around the rim of the bowl. But gradually the tiring team slowed, under the drag of the brake and the hands on the reins, then came to a panting stop. Only then could he turn his attention to Maita, and to this other grotesque figure of the Weasel who had risen up in time of need.

'Maita!' he choked, on his knees beside her. He raised her, and stilled with the wonder of it as her arms lifted, crept around his neck.

'Jim!' she whispered.

He held her for a moment, conscious that both of them were shivering with the reaction. He knew that he had only to hold her closer, and that she would respond—but this, of course, was the reaction of the moment, in being saved from what had threatened. An emotion which he couldn't afford to take advantage of. Once she had calmed, she would remember that he was not Professor Meader, but Gentleman Jim Thornton.

As she got unsteadily to her feet, he turned to the sprawled figure of the Weasel, his amazement increasing. The Weasel was lying there with his ankles tied together, one hand still pinioned behind his back. The other, the wrist raw and bleeding, was loose.

That was only a little of the blood. More of it stained his shirt front, bubbling freshly from a wound below the shoulder. This had been bandaged, but the bandage had slipped. There was a gag in his mouth as

well, and he shook his head as Gentleman
Jim pulled it loose.

'Thanks—Jim,' he gasped, but then, as
Gentleman Jim sought to adjust the
bandage again, shook his head.

'No good—with that, now,' he said. 'If
I'd kept quiet—it might have worked. Now
I'm—about finished. Which I guess is
lucky—for they won't get to hang me.'

Gentleman Jim eyed him, bewildered.

'We never liked each other, Weasel,' he
said. 'But it was sure fine of you to help the
way you did—'

'Fine, hell!' the Weasel snarled, with a
flash of his usual surliness. 'I'd of let you
take that jump, and willing, you dirty
double-crossin' skunk. You don't think I
did that for you, did you? Or for the skirt?'

'But you did it,' Gentleman Jim pointed
out.

'Yeah—to even with him!' the Weasel
growled. 'He was in that holdup at Red
Pine where my brother was killed—an'
helped to do it! That's how he knew
me—but I knew him!'

He sank back with a gasp, and it was
apparent that the jouncing ride, the fresh
breaking open of his wound, had been too
much. The Weasel wouldn't live to swing
from Hangman's Tree.

'I still appreciate it,' Gentleman Jim said
soberly. 'Whatever your reasons. But how'd

you get here—in this shape?'

The Weasel looked almost sheepish.

'It was that blasted Professor,' he explained. 'Big Nose left me behind to look after him and the little feller. I got what I figgered was a smart notion. I got hold of this sheep herder's outfit, figgerin' it was a lot like the Professor's, and loaded them in to start for town. And then—'

He paused, fighting for breath, but stubbornly determined to tell it.

'I guess I got careless. First thing I knew, Meader had got loose—I'd had him tied up, of course. I went at him with a knife—and somehow he turned it and it went in me. He didn't aim it that way. He fixed me up, and aimed to look after me—he's a good sort, kind of. They went off for a medico—and the next thing I knew, *he* come along and—and you know the rest—'

His voice ended abruptly, as the story was finished. So was the Weasel. And this, Gentleman Jim guessed, was the biggest piece of luck that had ever come the Weasel's way, even as with himself.

\*     \*     \*

The Professor's eyes twinkled. It was morning, and the town had, once again, a strangely peaceful appearance.

'You impressed me, at our first meeting,

as being quite a man, Jim,' Meader confessed. 'And I'm inclined more and more to that conviction as I learn more about you. The work you've done here is rather amazing. But I couldn't allow the impression to get abroad that you were the only one who could do things, could I? With my wound healed, I sort of had to demonstrate to all and sundry that I could do things for myself. That twisting knife was unfortunate.'

'But lucky for the Weasel, in the long run.'

'Maybe.' Meader's glance was quizzical, friendly. 'I had a bit of luck. But you sent word that you wanted to see me?'

'Yes. I—well, I started a job here—even if I didn't plan it that way. Then, of course, I kicked it all over, pretty much. What I was hoping was that you might sort of take things over and—and save something from the ruin, if you could. Let people know that there is an honest Professor who means what he says—'

'I think you convinced them of that, before I'd got here at all,' Meader said dryly. 'I'll do my best along those lines, of course, but I don't think you need much help. Here comes a sort of deputation now. And after what I've been hearing about you—my opinion is that they like you better than any audience has ever liked me.'

Gentleman Jim waited, uncertainly. He had expected a visit from the sheriff, but there had been none. He was coming now, however, and with him was John Gilson, Sam Staves and others of the business men.

'We have a definite promise that the railroad is going to come through here,' Gilson explained, with very little preamble. 'So, more than ever, we will need to build that church that we was talkin' about, and get us a sky pilot. And since Happy assures us that you could handle a building job as well as you do other things, Jim—why, we'd like to have you take charge of the job. Particularly since you raised the money for it.'

'Me?' For once in his life, Gentleman Jim was completely at a loss. True, he had had some building experience, in his years of knocking around, but this was an expression of confidence beyond his wildest dreams. 'After—after what has happened? As you know, I'm a wanted man—'

'*I* don't want you,' the sheriff protested. 'Except to help us out with a job, like they say. You promised to help clean up this town and make my job easier—and you've sure been a big help. A church ought to be right along the same lines, same as John Gilson figures, so I'm for it. As to the other—well, this is my bailiwick. Ain't no other law man goin' to come in here and interfere, not while I'm doin' the sheriffin'. Not that they would, anyway. I've been studyin'—seems, when it's boiled down, there ain't much against Gentleman Jim Thornton, anyway.'

Gentleman Jim swallowed uncertainly. Timothy Meader placed a hand on his shoulder.

'When you had a chance to get away with about twice as much money as you came here after, and took pains to save it for them—that would convince anybody,' he said. 'There's a big job to do here—for both of us. You're not the man to shirk because it will be a hard one.'

The others had gone, but Gentleman Jim became aware that Staves had lingered. He grinned uncertainly.

'Just thought you'd like a report on Happy,' he explained. 'Minerva found him and has him sobered up now. Happy swears he'll never touch another drop. And with Minerva to look after him—well, I rather fancy he'll have to keep to that.'

So Happy was to be given his chance as well. That, at least, was only simple justice. Minerva and Happy were made for each other. More to the point, he reflected, with a flash of his old spirit, it was a case of each for the other, or no one at all. Neither could be too choosy.

But as for himself—he was being treated

211

better than he deserved, far better than he had expected. But a man's past could not be so lightly brushed aside. Last night, Maita had been grateful. But she was young, beautiful, sister of the banker—

Sam Staves jostled his elbow, with the rough playfulness of a grizzly bear.

'They tell me you ain't been back to the Gilsons' for breakfast, not since yesterday,' he said. 'Um—well, I know about how you feel, I reckon. But take a look, man. I guess Maita's rememberin' what your step-daddy said about what your mother always did, when you was away and wanted back. The sun's two hours high, but it can still be seen plain—first time I've ever seen it that way, there—'

Gentleman Jim, looking where he pointed, drew in his breath sharply. Then he started to walk, slowly at first, but with increasing speed. There could be no mistake—not as to what it was, or what it meant. There was a lamp burning there, a light in the window. A light, he knew now, to lead him home.

212